CRUEL

THE BUCK BOYS HEROES SERIES

DEBORAH BLADON

FIRST ORIGINAL EDITION, 2022

eBook ISBN: 9781926440682
ISBN: 9798419847026

Book & cover design by Wolf & Eagle Media

deborahbladon.com

CHAPTER ONE

JULIET

"DO YOU HAVE PROTECTION?"

That question doesn't surprise me in the least. My older sister is always looking out for me. It's one of the reasons she bought this luxurious two-bedroom apartment in the heart of Tribeca.

Before she moved to New York City, I lived in a cramped room at an airport hotel. It was cheap and close to public transportation, so the commute to my workplace in midtown Manhattan was long but not horrible.

Living in Tribeca has made the trek to the office much more enjoyable.

It's even better for Margot. Since she relocated the offices of her lifestyle brand to the east coast from Los Angeles, it takes her less than five minutes to get to work.

Slipping on a faded denim jacket over my white eyelet blouse, I glance in her direction.

Margot is old-school-movie-star beautiful.

Her blonde hair is usually styled in a flawless French twist. Her blue eyes are always rimmed with just the right amount of eyeliner and mascara.

Her best friend, who works as a chemist at one of the country's premier cosmetic companies, formulated a lipstick shade for Margot for her birthday. It's called Crimson Plum, and when I tried a sample, I admit I looked like a clown.

I can't pull off bright red lipstick, but on Margot, it only adds to her allure.

I stick with pale shades for my lips, black mascara to accentuate my hazel eyes, and loose waves for my long brown hair.

"I don't need protection," I assure her as I wrap my black and white polka dot scarf around my neck. "I'll be fine, Margie."

She sticks out the tip of her tongue the way she always does when I use her childhood nickname. "You have that whistle I gave you, don't you? And you remember all those moves we learned in the self-defense class we took together?"

I strike a pose with my arms stretched in front of me and one knee bent in the air. I tilt my head and plaster on the scariest expression I can muster. "This was one of them, right?"

Margot shakes her head. "I'd run for the hills if I saw you on the street doing that."

I straighten my knee and drop both hands to my hips. "I'm good then."

"I'm coming with you," she announces, dragging herself off the couch. "I can watch this episode later."

"No," I say loudly enough that it stops my sister in her tracks.

She's wearing sweatpants and a concert tour T-shirt. Her hair is tangled in a mess around her shoulders.

Margot is the epitome of style. She only digs out her comfortable clothes and turns off her phone when she needs a break from the high pressure of her job.

"What?" she questions with widening eyes. "I can come with you if I want, Juliet."

I refuse to allow her to interrupt her mini staycation to trudge to midtown Manhattan with me. By tomorrow morning, she'll be back in the trenches, running her multi-million dollar company. Tonight, I want her to be Margie Bardin, lover of period romances. Sitting in front of the television, binge-watching her latest obsession that is chock-full of dukes and duchesses, is where she needs to be.

She approaches me with hurried steps until she's standing right in front of me.

"Remember what dad taught us." She holds out her hand. "Give me your keys so I can give you a refresher before you leave."

I dig my keys out of the front pocket of my black jeans and deposit them in her palm even though I've never forgotten the trick our father taught us when I was fifteen and Margot was eighteen. It may have been ten years ago, but it feels like yesterday.

She gathers the keys in her fist before the blade of one of my keys peeks out from between two of her fingers like a mini jagged knife. "Do this if anyone tries to mug you, Juliet."

I nod.

She lunges toward me with three stabbing motions. "Jab, jab, cut."

I hold in a laugh because Margot can't pull off the tough-as-nails, badass-fighter look.

"Show me," she says, pushing the keys back at me.

Not wanting to keep the man I'm meeting waiting, I play

along to appease her concern by mimicking her motions. "Jab, jab, slash."

"Ohhh," her voice trails. "I like that better."

I pocket my keys and steal a glance around the living room in search of my purse. "I have to run, Margie."

"I'll turn on my phone because I need you to call me as soon as he gives you what you want."

"Why don't you ever say that after I go on a date?" I wink.

She scrunches her nose. "Let me believe you're a virgin for at least the next ten years."

"I'm not," I say with a grin. "But, I'll play along if it makes you feel better."

"A quick knee to the groin is almost as good as the key trick."

"Got it." I take her in my arms for a hug. "I won't be more than an hour. I'll meet my informant, find out what he has for me, and pick us up a pint of ice cream on my way home."

"Mint chocolate chip?" She asks with a perk of one of her perfectly arched eyebrows.

"Done." I move to kiss her cheek. "Have fun watching the Duke get downright dirty."

"He does not," she scoffs. "Or he won't in the episode I'm about to watch. It's the third of this season."

"I'm on the sixth," I admit. "The third and the fourth are H.O.T., and for the record, his full-frontal nude scene is spectacular."

She looks toward the television. "Go do what you need to do, Juliet. I have a show to watch."

CHAPTER TWO

JULIET

I STEP out of an Uber on Madison Avenue. I would have taken the subway, but my sister's mini self-defense course ate up a bit of my time. That, along with a conversation I had with one of the doormen of our building, set me back by fifteen minutes.

Ricky, the doorman, had a host of questions for me about an online article I wrote two weeks ago. He's always telling me he's my number one fan. I take pride in my work, even if this job isn't my ultimate end goal. It's a step up the ladder toward the future I desperately want.

I spot the man I'm meeting right away.

He insists that I refer to him as my informant, but I see him as a helpful aid in my pursuit of the meat and bones of the stories I'm assigned.

"Juliet!" he yells my name while waving a hand in my direction.

For an *informant*, there is nothing discreet about Bradley Degati.

A waft of purple hair sits atop the middle of his head. His brown eyes are behind a pair of orange-rimmed eyeglasses, and the suits he wears are never the standard navy blue or black. Today, it's powder blue with a red vest. His pants are always hemmed a few inches too short, so that he can show off his colorful socks.

"Hey, Brad." I smile as I approach him.

He gives me a big bear hug. "You're looking fantastic tonight."

I spin in a circle on the crowded sidewalk. "Thank you. I'm liking your look too."

"This little number," he says, tugging on the sleeve of his jacket. "Trudy found this in a vintage store. I swear I married the greatest stylist on this continent."

I have to agree with him.

Trudy Degati's personality and presence are just as infectious as her husband's.

"Do you have something good for me?" I ask with hope.

I've been chasing a big story all week, and when I shared those details with Brad, he told me he'd do his best to help me out. When he called me an hour ago to ask me to meet him outside of a restaurant, I knew that it had to be good news.

"Let's take this around the corner," he suggests.

I go along for the walk because it's become part of our routine. When we do the exchange of money for information, Brad prefers that it be on a side street or in a mostly-empty café.

We step into a narrow alleyway between two brick buildings.

His hand dives into the inner pocket of his suit jacket. He tugs out a flash drive. "Pictures! I have pictures!"

"You don't," I say in disbelief. "How? When?"

"I do." He laughs. "Someone took the pictures this morning at their studio."

Someone is code for Trudy.

Brad has never come right out and admitted it, but the trail to his source isn't long and winding. His wife works with some of the biggest names in entertainment, and many social media influencers, including a particular one who is rumored to be on the cusp of an engagement with her recently retired NFL superstar boyfriend.

"You're telling me you have pictures of Corla Berletti's engagement ring?" I lower my voice. "Actual pictures of the ring?"

"Fucking amazing pictures of the ring, if I do say so myself." He brushes a hand over his shoulder. "I'm talking high definition. You can almost feel the weight of all ten carats when you look at the photos."

My jaw drops. "Ten carats?"

"Princess cut, and a white gold band engraved with his initials. Corla might have taken the ring off briefly this morning when she was trying on a wool dress. I'm not confirming that mind you, but the possibility exists. So you're getting pictures of the ring on and off her finger. You're welcome."

I plant both hands on Brad's shoulders, push up to the tiptoes of my boots, and kiss his cheek. "Thank you."

Stepping back, I slip the strap of my purse over my head so I can dig out the money I brought with me.

"Did your sister insist you tie yourself up in the strap of that bag?" Brad chuckles.

"Of course she did," I say with a laugh. "She won't let me

leave home without it wrapped around me like a crossbody bag. She doesn't get that the strap is too short for that, so I always feel like my chest is being crushed."

He holds out a hand. "The strap can be lengthened. Let me do that."

Shaking my head, I sigh. "I want to pay you first. I brought five hundred cash. That works, right?"

He nods. "It's going directly into our Maui mad money account."

Brad is saving the money I give him for a surprise trip to Maui for his and Trudy's fifth wedding anniversary.

He works for a firm on Wall Street. He's convinced that the stress of that will melt into the sand in Hawaii when he's sunning himself next to his wife and sipping on a tropical drink.

I slide the money out from a zippered compartment within my purse.

I hand him the cash just as he slips me the flash drive. I tuck it away in the same zippered compartment for safe-keeping since it's worth more than its weight in gold.

"It's always a pleasure doing business with you, Juliet." Shoving the money into his pocket, he smiles. "Give me the purse so I can fix the strap before I run. I'm meeting Trudy for dinner. I'd invite you, but it's romantic, and you would be…"

"I'd be the third wheel," I finish his thought.

He makes quick work of the strap, adjusting it so it's a few inches longer. "You'll be able to breathe now and still make your sister happy."

I take the purse back. "You're a lifesaver."

His phone chimes in his pocket. He yanks it out to look at the screen. "It's my beauty queen. She's already at the restaurant. I need to run."

Before I can say a word, his back is turned to me as he sprints out of the alley.

My gaze trails him. “Thanks again, Brad!”

“You’re welcome, sunshine,” he calls back before he disappears out of view.

I take stock of where I am.

If I cut through the alley, I’ll be on the same street that houses the ice cream shop that Juliet loves.

She claims that they make the best mint chocolate chip in the city. Since she almost always eats the entire pint when I bring one home, I trust her opinion more than my own.

I start in the direction of the store as I dig my phone out of my purse to send my sister a text telling her that I made it through my meeting in one piece.

Without warning, I feel a sharp and sudden tug on the strap of my purse.

It’s dangling at my side, but it doesn’t take me more than a second to realize that there is a hand wrapped around it that doesn’t belong to me.

The hand is large and covered with a dusting of dark hair.

Panic darts through me as I tuck the purse close to me, trying to counter the man’s strength.

“No!” I scream. “Stop!”

He lets out a grunt, and before I can fathom what’s happening, I’m struck with a pain in the back of my head that takes me to the ground.

CHAPTER THREE

JULIET

THE THROBBING in the back of my head is losing the war against the biting pain coming from the left side of my forehead.

I'm still holding tightly to my purse even though I'm on my side on the concrete. I'm determined not to let the big ogre standing in front of me steal it away.

"Get lost!" I scream up at him.

He bares his teeth as if that's going to scare me. "Give it to me," he snarls.

"No!" I kick at him, trying to ward him off as he yanks harder and harder on the strap.

With one final tug, the purse slips from my hands, sending almost everything inside of it onto the ground around me.

Suddenly, the guy stumbles forward, and his hands fly in the air. He crashes onto the pavement less than a foot from where I am.

I inch back on my ass in a desperate attempt to get away from him.

"Leave her the fuck alone." A man's deep voice catches me off guard. "What the hell is wrong with you?"

The mugger is on his knees trying to get up, but he's knocked down onto his side, pulling a loud wailing sound from him.

"Give me your scarf." The mysterious voice overpowers the whimpering coming from the assailant.

Unable to resist the temptation to see the face attached to that mesmerizing voice, I look up.

I come face-to-face with utter perfection in a black suit.

Inky black hair that brushes the collar of his black shirt, blue eyes, and full lips greet me. His Greek God nose and chiseled jawline suits everything else on his model-worthy face.

I've seen gorgeous men before, but this man blows all of them out of the water.

"What?" I whisper.

"Give me your scarf," he says again, pausing between each word. "Now."

I quickly tug my scarf free and offer it to him, all while the man who tried to steal my purse is writhing on the ground, being held in place by one of the brutally handsome man's hands.

He flips the guy onto his stomach and skillfully ties his hands behind his back with my scarf.

The blue-eyed stranger stares at me. "Feel free to call 911 at any point."

Fumbling my way through a thank you, I manage to press the emergency button on my phone.

"I'm… he… my purse," I spit out between staggered breaths to the woman who answered.

The man who rescued me looks in my direction. "Tell them it's an attempted robbery, and the assailant is subdued for now."

I repeat each of his words into my phone and then follow that with the directions he calls out to me.

"I'm sending a patrol car right away, Ma'am," the 911 operator explains in a reassuring tone. "Did you suffer any injuries?"

Shaking my head, I reach up to run my fingers over my forehead. I immediately feel something wet. "Oh, no. I think I'm bleeding. I broke my fall with my shoulder, but my head hit the pavement."

"I'll dispatch the paramedics as well," she says. "Please stay on the line."

Without any thought, I end the call.

I glance at my hand, and even under the dim light illuminating the darkened alley, I can tell that it is indeed blood.

"Don't move, asshole." The mysterious stranger gazes down at the man he tied up before he shifts his attention to me. "Are you all right?"

I lock eyes with him, but it's so intense that I drop my gaze to the ground around me.

I realize that almost everything from my purse is strewn around me.

"My stuff," I whisper. "I need to pick it up."

Tugging out his pocket square, he dabs the soft fabric on my forehead. "You're bleeding. You need to stay put."

"I'm fine," I insist as I start to reach for my belongings.

The guy on the ground catches my eye. "If I'm arrested for this, you're going to pay for it."

The mysterious stranger snaps his head toward the man. "Shut the fuck up. If you go anywhere near her again in this lifetime, I will personally hunt you down, and I promise you'll regret it."

I grab a tube of lipstick and my MetroCard. I try to extend my reach more, but I'm suddenly struck with a wave of dizziness.

"Sit still," the handsome stranger instructs me in a curt tone.

Before I can argue, he's scooped up most of my things.

He shoves them at me but holds tight to a red lanyard attached to a press pass from a concert I covered in the summer.

I watch in silence as he studies it.

His eyes dart to my face as soon as sirens approach from the distance. He hands me the press pass along with his pocket square. "It's still bleeding. Apply pressure until you get to the hospital."

"I'm fine, " I whisper.

His dark hair halos his face as he stares into my eyes. He takes my hand to guide the pocket square to my forehead. "Apply pressure."

Nodding, I manage a weak smile. "Thank you for helping me."

He doesn't acknowledge those words. Instead, he turns back to the man who tried to mug me. He leans close to him, whispers something in his ear, and then just as I catch sight of the reflection of the red and blue flashing lights of a police car on a window at the end of the alleyway, the handsome stranger takes off in a sprint in the opposite direction.

"Wait," I call after him. "Please don't leave me alone with him."

"With me?"

I glance at the man who assaulted me as I inch away from him. I fully expect him to try and scramble to his feet to make a run for it at any second now that the police car has come to a stop and two officers are rushing toward us.

"You're safer with me than you were with that guy that rammed his shoe into the back of my knees."

Before I can ask what the hell he's talking about, a police officer is pulling him up to his feet, while another asks me if I'm okay.

The reality of what happened finally hits me full force, and with a single tear trailing down my cheek, I tell her I'll be all right. I know I will be. I've lived through far worse than this.

CHAPTER FOUR

JULIET

"JULIET," Margot's voice breaks the moment she rounds the corner to find me in an exam room in the emergency department at Lennox Hill Hospital.

"I'm all right," I reassure her immediately with an outstretched hand. "I'm totally fine, Margie."

She rushes to take me into her arms.

I wince at the strength of her grip as she hugs me. "I was so scared."

Those are words that haven't left her lips in years. Margot rarely cries. She's stoic and strong, and when disaster strikes, she's always the first to approach the issue with a level head.

This is different, though. The spots of blood that are staining the front of my blouse prove that I was injured at some point since she last saw me.

I didn't tell her that on the phone.

I wouldn't have told her anything, but the doctor who

examined me explained that I'd need someone to accompany me home.

The cut on my forehead wasn't deep enough for stitches, and according to him, I don't have a concussion, but the dizziness I experienced in the alley and again when I tried getting up from the stretcher was enough to concern him.

I called Margie then and told her I'd fallen and was at the hospital being checked to make sure that nothing was broken.

"What exactly happened?" she asks just as the doctor walks back into the room.

"Juliet is a crime fighting hero," he blurts out.

Dr. Gavin Fuller may be good-looking and have a great bedside manner, but he's terrible at upholding doctor-patient confidentiality. I saw him talking to the paramedics who brought me in.

"What?" Margot's head snaps in his direction. "What are you talking about?"

The dark-haired doctor looks to me for guidance. Since he let the cat out of the bag, I try and shove it back in. "He's making a joke."

The serious look on his face doesn't play into my charade, and it takes all of one second for my sister to notice that.

She turns her attention back to me. "Juliet. I want you to tell me right now what the hell happened."

"Language," I warn her with a smile. "There are children here, Margot. I saw them bring in a pregnant woman. She had her sweet little daughter with her. She stopped to talk to me in the waiting room."

"You're stalling," my sister accuses. "Don't do that."

She's right. I am stalling because telling Margot that I was mugged will send her back to California, and she'll drag me with her.

"She stopped an assailant." Dr. Fuller continues his quest to inject himself into our conversation. "She tied up a mugger with her scarf."

What the fuck?

My gaze lands on him. "Doctor…"

"My cousin is a detective with the NYPD," he explains to my sister. "He called me a few minutes ago to see how Juliet is doing. The man in the alley confessed to an attempted mugging. Juliet tied him up. She restrained him until the police arrived."

Margot's hand jumps to cover her mouth. "Oh my god."

"She deserves a medal for catching one of the bad guys." He shoots me a megawatt smile.

"Juliet." Margot takes my hand. "You're so brave."

I want her to believe that. I want her to see that in me because I know she values courage more than almost anything else.

"What about the woman he mugged?" she questions me. "Is she all right?"

"She's fine," Dr. Fuller answers. "She'll be a little sore for a day or two and might sport a few bruises, but thankfully, her arm broke her fall, so she's good. She's really good."

"I'M CONFUSED," I confess to Dr. Fuller when Margot leaves the exam room to order an Uber.

"Confused as in you don't know your name or…"

"Confused as in why didn't you tell my sister the whole story?"

He offers a hand for me to slide off the exam table. "What part did I leave out?"

I take his hand to stand. "You know what part."

"Do I?"

I look up at his face. "You do."

"The paramedic explained what the mugger told him when he was checking him out for injuries." He motions to my hands. "You tied him up with your scarf. You were hurt in that scuffle. My cousin backed that story up."

"He did?"

"They got a full confession out of the guy at the police station," he goes on, "I suspect you're talking about the identity of the woman he accosted."

I nod in silence.

"Your sister was scared," he says quietly. "I was outside the room when she arrived. I heard the fear in her voice. I sense she'd take it a lot harder if she knew you were the woman he mugged."

"She would."

"It's not my place to tell her that you defended yourself like a champ because he was trying to nab your purse." He looks down at the tablet in his hands. "If or when you think she needs to know that, you'll tell her, but that's between the two of you."

Still confused as to why he keeps saying I took down the mugger myself, I sigh.

"New York City is a great place." He smiles. "A few assholes are lurking about, but for the most part, the rest of us are the cream of the crop. Do what you need to do to put this behind you. If you'd like to speak to someone about it, I can recommend one of the best."

I smile, grateful that he's intuitive enough to know the impact that today had on me. "Thank you, but I'll be all right. I'm resilient."

"You're also someone I'd want coaching me in a boxing

ring." He laughs. "Pop a couple of ibuprofen later if you need them to help ease the head pain."

"I will."

"Other than that, you're good to go." He pats my forearm. "Take care of yourself and anyone else who needs it."

I let out a squeak of a laugh. "I'll try my best."

CHAPTER FIVE

JULIET

AN HOUR LATER, I take a seat on the edge of my bed and let the weight of the last few hours settle over me.

As soon as we got home from the hospital, Margot insisted on making me a cup of tea.

I don't drink tea. She does.

To appease her anxiety, I dutifully sipped from the mug of green tea she prepared for me. I would have preferred a tequila shot, but I knew, deep in my heart, that my sister felt a need to take care of me.

She made small talk about her work and the weather and then retold a story about the first dog we ever owned.

It's her go-to when she's overwhelmed.

She'll retreat to a childhood memory that comforts her.

After I finished half of the tea, I told her I needed a shower, and after a two minute long hug, she finally let me go.

A light knock on my bedroom door lures my gaze in that direction. "What is it, Margie?"

The door slowly opens a crack. "I forgot to ask if you want to watch the show with me when you're done your shower. I'll skip ahead to episode six for you."

I smile when I catch sight of her face as she peers around the half-open door.

"I can circle back to the other episodes another time."

"I love that you'd be willing to do that for me." I smile. "I think I'm going to turn in after my shower. I have a big story to work on tomorrow, so I want to get an early start on that."

It's true, but I need a moment to breathe on my own.

I need time to decompress and absorb what happened so I can put it behind me and wake up in the morning ready to face the day.

"I get it," she says. "I'll probably watch one more episode and hit the hay too."

I nod. "I love you. Sleep well."

"Love you," she bounces back. "Dream good dreams, okay?"

"I will," I reassure her.

As soon as she's shut the door again, I dive my hand into the pockets of my denim jacket. It's a standard move since my sister often comes into my room to collect laundry, even though I've told her time and time again that I can handle it on my own.

My fingers brush against something soft, and for the first time since I left the alley on a stretcher, I remember the stranger's pocket square.

I tug it out of my pocket.

Three red dots of my blood are a startling contrast against the light gray silk. I trace a fingertip over one of the dots, but it's dried now.

I flip the pocket square over to find two letters embroidered into the fabric in a shade of thread not much darker than the silk itself.

K.B.

I bring it closer to get a better look.

The lingering scent of cologne on the silk stirs something within me. I hold the pocket square to my nose and inhale deeply.

It's a warm scent, spiced with musk and woodsy notes.

It's delicious and inviting and conjures up an image of the stranger and his brilliant blue eyes, and carved from stone features.

"K.B.," I whisper the letters as I trace a finger over them. "Who are you?"

In a metropolis this vast, with millions of people filling its more intimate corners, the chances of me ever running into him again are slim to none.

I tell myself that, yet at the same time, I make a mental note to take the pocket square to the dry cleaners on the off chance that one day I'll come face to face with my savior again.

"YOU OUTDID YOURSELF, JULIET." My boss beams as he reads over the rough draft of my next story.

Smiling, I nod. "You know how much I love the feel good articles."

"Feel good?" Pushing back from his desk, he stands. "They're great, but they don't rake in the ad dollars, do they?"

I know it.

I've heard it time and time again.

My job as a writer for one of the most popular gossip blogs in the country should be something I'm proud of. When I landed the interview with RumorMel, I saw it as a way to get my foot in the door at Marks Creative.

Marks is a global multi-media company that runs many magazines and websites. It's also the driving force behind a cable network.

I'm most interested in one particular publication that falls under Marks' umbrella. New York Viewpoint is a news magazine with digital and printed subscription rates totaling tens of millions.

I read my first copy of the magazine last year, and I was hooked. Before that, I had earned a degree in journalism from UCLA, edited a community newspaper, and worked for two regional digital news outlets in Anaheim.

Being offered the job at RumorMel meant a step up the ladder toward my future. That's how I view it.

Melburn Meekes, the namesake of the website, is nearing ninety now. He started reporting celebrity gossip in a column in a national newspaper more than sixty years ago. He still checks in occasionally, but since he sold his brand to Marks, it's under the direction of my boss, Hugo Conall.

"Give this another sprinkle of your magic touch, and I'll post it within the hour," Hugo says as he scans my face. "What happened to your forehead, Juliet?"

I run a finger over the bandage I put on when I was getting ready for work this morning.

I tried styling my hair to cover it. I was going for a long bangs look but couldn't get my hair to stay in place. I finally gave up and decided if asked, I'd come up with an explanation that is short and sweet. The problem with that is I'm drawing a blank.

"Don't tell me." He huffs out a laugh. "You drank a few

too many celebratory shots after you scored those pictures. The next thing you know, you ran straight into a wall that you didn't remember was always there."

Unsure of what to say, I smile.

"It happens to the best of us." He runs a finger along his chin. "I wrote a breaking story twenty years ago that left me with a long scar right about here."

I've noticed that scar. I thought it added character to his face. I had no idea it was the result of a night of drinking.

"Spruce this up." He hands the paper I printed my article on back to me. "I want it online for the masses by the time they sit down for lunch."

CHAPTER SIX

KAVAN

"ARE YOU NURSING A BROKEN HEART, BANE?"

I look to my right to catch sight of a man I didn't invite here. Unfortunately, Sean Wells shows up at the most inopportune times. It's a habit of his. I consider it a bad habit that started when we met as teenagers at The Buchanan School. It's an elite boarding school upstate funded by the outrageous tuition that New York State's most influential parents happily pay so their sons can carry the burden of being Buchanan alum on their shoulders forever.

"What the hell are you talking about?" I question as he sits his ass on the barstool next to me.

"You were checking out the breaking news about Corla Berletti's engagement ring." He taps his fingertip on the edge of my phone case. "That rock she's wearing beats the one Graham got Trina."

The mention of our mutual friend and his wife brings my

gaze up to Sean's face. I focus on his brown eyes. "Graham did all right."

He nods. "He has a beautiful wife he adores. I'd say he's doing better than all right, Kavan."

Graham Locke fake married his assistant to appease the wishes of a man he considers a father. As they navigated through that, they fell in love.

Judging by the peace that has settled over Graham that worked out for him.

"Don't try and change the subject." Sean thumps his closed fist against the wooden bar luring the bartender's gaze in our direction.

The guy offers Sean a curt nod. That tells me that he knows exactly what Sean wants. I do as well. Scotch neat and preferably the most expensive label they offer.

"What subject?" I question him as he tugs on the lapels of his suit jacket.

"The one about you reading an article on RumorMel." A hearty laugh chases the words out of him. "I never would have pinned you for a Melster, Bane."

"What the fuck is a Melster?"

He points a finger at my face. "I'm looking at one."

I raise both brows in silent question.

"It's someone addicted to that damn website." He shakes his head. "Melsters crave details about famous people."

Swiping a finger over my phone's screen to close the browser, I return my attention to the almost empty glass in front of me. "Why are you here?"

"Why are you reading RumorMel?" He chuckles. "Look, Bane, I'm not dropping this because it's too good. You're the last person I expected to catch reading gossip."

I haven't explained any of my actions to another person in years. I sure as hell won't start tonight.

"Thanks," Sean directs that to the bartender as he slides a glass of scotch in front of him. "Top up his with the same."

I don't get in the middle of that because I could use another drink and a few minutes with Sean.

He's one of three men I consider friends. I'd never admit that to any of them, but Graham, Sean, and Harrison Keene have stood by my side since I was a fifteen-year-old kid navigating my way through a family battle.

They witnessed the height of that and the aftermath when my life fractured before I worked to piece it back together.

"How's the Trade Minds deal going?" Sean tosses that out there and then takes a drink.

"Dead in the water," I say with an even tone. "They backed out last week."

Scratching his beard-covered chin, he glances around the almost empty bar. "You're shitting me, right?"

I wish I were.

I can't deny that acquiring Trade Minds would have been a huge win for Bane Enterprises as the plan was to merge the technology firm with the company we acquired several years ago. That would have strengthened our position in the market as we set out to launch a new line of products, including smartphones, laptops, and security devices.

Technology is only one branch of the business we do, but it's worth investing in. I view this as a setback but not one that's insurmountable.

"They didn't like your terms, did they?" He chuckles. "You need to learn how to negotiate. When was the last time you gave an inch, Bane?"

Five years ago, I gave much more than an inch. I sacrificed everything for someone.

I take a drink from the newly filled glass in front of me.

"Back at Buchanan, you would have cracked a joke about my dick if I asked about giving me an inch."

I stare straight ahead. "Back at Buchanan, you were working with an inch, maybe an inch and a half. If memory serves, it took some time for you to mature."

"Your memory is failing you, Kavan. I've always had more than most women can handle. I'm talking eight and a half very satisfying and thick…" He trails off, nudging my elbow with his.

I turn to glance in his direction to catch a smirk on his lips as his hand threads through his brown hair. He wiggles both brows in silence.

"One more word about your dick, and our friendship is over, Sean."

He takes a mouthful of his drink and swallows it. "Agreed if you tell me why you were on RumorMel. Are you buying the site?"

"Is it for sale?" I ask, amused that he's not giving up his hunt to get to the bottom of why I was scouring that website when he walked in.

"Everything and everyone is for sale," he quips. "Name a price. I bet old Mel would take you up on that offer."

He might if he hadn't sold the enterprise to Marks Creative several years ago.

Sean may have caught me reading a story about a social media star I've never heard of and the hideous ring her athlete boyfriend bought her, but I have no interest in any of those people.

I'm curious about the woman who penned that piece.

Juliet Bardin.

I saved her from being mugged last week, and then I took the necessary steps to keep my name out of that complication.

It was the right move considering the fact that Miss Bardin earns a living reporting on the lives of people in the public eye, and I work very hard to avoid the spotlight.

CHAPTER SEVEN

KAVAN

I'M NOT a man who permits anyone to back him into a corner.

I'm always aware of my surroundings, including my position now.

Nigel Rothe, my late father's right-hand man and current personal advisor to me, is standing in front of my desk with his gaze trained on one of the many windows in my office that overlooks Manhattan.

"The board isn't going to drop this, Mr. Bane."

It doesn't matter how many times I've insisted that he call me by my first name. Nigel is old school and loyal to his core.

He worked for my father for many years, and as soon as I took the reins of the company, he accepted the advisor position. It's impossible for me to remember a time when Nigel wasn't a prominent part of my life.

He's right about the board of directors.

I spent the bulk of the afternoon in a meeting with the group. Each of them took their turn explaining what they perceived as the root cause of the declining price of Bane Enterprises stock and the core reason Trade Minds backed out of our agreement.

I wasn't surprised when every finger came back pointing at me.

All of the dozens of books written about me over the past few years that professed to contain '*firsthand knowledge*' of my life or '*gruesome (never before heard) details*' about the night the Bane family changed forever are bullshit.

That includes the one released just last week with the uninspired title of *The Bad Bane*. It's currently topping every bestseller list.

Add that to the never-ending list of podcasts that have made a fortune focusing on me and the articles posted online written by supposed insiders, and I can see why the board views me as the issue.

"You don't think that once the hype of this latest book dies down that they'll retreat?" My question is rhetorical since stock prices have fallen steadily since I took on the position of CEO two years ago.

Nigel closes his eyes briefly. It's a telltale sign that he's drawing on the never-ending reservoir of patience that sits within him. "I know the board, sir. I've known some of them longer than…"

"I've been alive," I interrupt. "I'm aware."

"They sent me a private memo." He taps the screen of his phone. "The shareholders made it very clear to the board that they want one thing."

Nigel won't go there. He refuses to, but I will, so I do. "They want a mea culpa for what happened in Miami. They want me to put all of my cards on the table."

Nigel's blue eyes scan my face in search of something. He won't find whatever he's looking for because I've learned how to bury the past in a grave so deep that it can never be unearthed by anyone.

"It's a dark cloud that's been hanging over Bane Enterprises for many years." His voice has a tremor in it as he continues, "I do so wish you'd let me talk to the press or perhaps a ghostwriter. I can work on a memoir with someone under the guise that you wrote it, of course. That would clear all of this up, and I imagine a project like that would send stock prices on an upward trajectory."

I shoot him a look that he knows all too well.

I've never told Nigel to shut the fuck up, but that look says what I can't.

"The police then," he rattles on. "They could handle revealing all to the press if I go to them with the information we've withheld."

"Nigel." His name comes out like a thinly veiled warning. "That's not happening."

He nods in agreement. "Very well, sir."

I move to stand. Buttoning my suit jacket, I round my desk. "If anyone is going to speak to the press, it'll be me."

"You?" He doesn't try to hide the surprise in his tone. "You swore never to speak of that night."

"I'm not talking about that night."

That fucking night when the world fell off its axis in the darkness with rain pouring down in buckets and the angry roar of thunder punctuating the moment.

"What then?"

"I will agree to speak to a journalist of my choosing about my vision for the company's future," I propose. "The board will see that the article will strengthen Bane's position as a global brand, and it will quiet their fears that my past will continue to impact what my father worked so hard to build."

Nigel studies me carefully as he pushes his wire-rimmed eyeglasses up the bridge of his nose. "Drown out the past with the promise of a brighter undeniable tomorrow? That might work. I know a reporter with The Times. He's very well respected. He'll go deep, but you can warn him of the subjects that you feel are off-limits."

I shake my head. "No. I have someone in mind."

Someone I can easily guide to write an article that will not reveal anything beyond what I want.

I don't need a seasoned journalist poking my brain with their manipulative questions. I have no doubt that I can navigate that with ease, but the last thing I want is a headline screaming about my refusal to answer anything.

If I control the narrative of the interview, I can finally shift the focus from my past to the company's future.

It will change nothing for me, but perhaps, it will shake off some of the stigmas that have been haunting Bane Enterprises since I took over.

"May I ask who?" Nigel quizzes.

Now is not the time to tell him that my plan is for the article to appear in New York Viewpoint since I know that Thurston Marks, the owner of Marks Creative, would walk barefoot over hot coals to get an exclusive from me. Surely, he won't have an issue with my choice of a journalist.

"Send a secret memo back to the board that I'm ready to sit down for a magazine article," I accentuate the word *secret* because the concept is laughable. I'm aware of every electronic communication that takes place within this company. "Then we'll begin the process of securing the journalist I have in mind."

Journalist. Gossip Columnist. Reporter.

Whatever Juliet Bardin chooses to call herself is fine with me.

Her expertise is writing articles about the size of engagement rings.

I'm about to drop her into the middle of the ocean with a shark circling her. If she follows my rules, I won't bite...hard.

CHAPTER EIGHT

JULIET

"WHO WANTS TO SPEAK TO ME?" I ask Hugo as he stands in front of my desk.

He leans closer to lower his voice so my co-workers in the cubicles around me won't hear him. "Mr. Marks."

I study his lips to see if the movement matches the name that just fell from them.

It's not that I can read lips. I can't, but somewhere between Hugo's mouth and my ears, the name he said got jumbled because there's no way that owner of Marks Creative wants to talk to me.

I'm one of the lowest-ranked employees on staff.

Hugo has tried to boost my confidence by telling me that I'm the lead junior writer for RumorMel. That would mean a lot more if there were other junior writers on staff.

I'm the only one. My co-workers have all been working the job for at least two years. I just passed the six month mark.

I glance down at the pink and red floral dress I'm wearing. I would have paired it with something other than my black leather jacket and low-heeled black boots if I knew I was going to have an audience with the owner of the company.

"Juliet," Hugo stresses my name. "You need to come with me now. Mr. Marks is waiting for you."

I stay seated behind my desk because I don't have any confidence that my legs will work at this moment. That's because my knees are shaking. "Why?"

"Why what?" He shoves a hand through his red curly hair.

"Why does he want to see me?" I narrow my eyes. "Did I mess up? Was it the pictures of Corla Berletti's engagement ring? My source has been supplying me with information for months. I can't reveal who it is, though. If that means I'm going to lose this job, so be it. I have to stick by my principles."

I can tell that he's fighting to hold in a smile. "I'm impressed with your loyalty to Brad, but this isn't about those pictures."

That jolts me to my feet. "You know Brad?"

He laughs. "How do you think Brad found you?"

I assumed it was my call out on social media for anyone with information on my first story. That involved a lost poodle that belonged to a Broadway star. Brad sent me a cryptic message about a doggie in a window with a snapshot of a poodle in the window of a townhouse on the Upper East Side.

I followed that tip and found the dog.

The woman who owned the townhouse lived a block from the Broadway star and took the dog in on a snowy night.

She'd already reached out to the dog's owner by the time I showed up on her stoop.

Still, I met up with Brad at a coffee shop, slipped him one hundred dollars for his help, and we became fast friends.

"You sent him my way," I say with a slight grin. "That's why you always approve my petty cash requests for my informant."

"Brad is either a one hundred or five hundred dollar source even though he could be charging ten or twenty times that." He smirks. "He's been lending us a hand for a few years now."

I sigh. "He's fun to work with."

"Very," Hugo agrees with a nod. "Are you ready, Juliet?"

That yanks me back to this moment in time and the meeting I'm supposed to attend.

I round my desk. "Do you know why Mr. Marks wants to see me?"

He nods. "I do, but he wants to explain the reason to you."

I fall in step behind him as we head toward the elevator. The executive offices of Marks Creative are on the top floor of this office tower.

RumorMel's offices are five floors below.

Hugo jabs his finger into the elevator call button. "You have something special, Juliet."

I glance at him. "What do you mean?"

"Your drive." He smiles, and it carries to his kind blue eyes. "You remind me of myself when I was first starting out."

"That means a lot to me, Hugo."

He nods. "I'm glad to see your forehead healed up just fine, but you might need another bandage after this meeting."

As cryptic as that is, I piece it together just as the elevator doors slide open. "You think I'm going to be in a celebratory mood after this meeting."

Waving me ahead of him so I can board the lift first, he grins. "I know you will be."

As the doors slide shut behind us after he pushes the button for the top floor, I glance at his profile. "Is that the only hint I'm getting?"

"You're the investigative journalist." He perks both of his eyebrows. "Surely, you can draw your own conclusion based on the clues I've dropped."

I look up to see the numbers edging up as we make our journey to Mr. Marks's office. "It's really good news, isn't it?"

He leans closer to drop his voice to a whisper. "You didn't hear it from me, but yes. It is damn good news for you."

CHAPTER NINE

JULIET

WE STEP off the elevator on the executive floor of Marks Creative, and I need a second to take it all in.

I thought my sister's offices were beautiful, but this puts them to shame.

The floor is polished stone. The reception desk is crafted from steel with sleek edges. The lighting is muted, but the fixtures themselves are breathtaking.

"Wow," I whisper.

"I know, right?" Hugo shoots me a look. "The first time I was called up here, I snapped a few pictures for my wife. She's an interior designer."

I take one last glance to the left and then the right before my gaze lands on the man behind the reception desk. I suck in a deep breath. "Is it show time, Hugo?"

"It is," he says, gesturing to the right. "They're waiting for us, so let's head in."

I turn to look at him. "They?"

Hugo moves a hand, so it's hovering just inches from my arm. "We need to get in there, Juliet."

Nodding, I start in the direction I know we're headed. "I wish I would have worn something else today."

Hugo chuckles. "You look great. Stylish with a little edge."

I glance down at my dress. "I guess that's one way to put it."

Smiling, he leads me around a corner past an open area where many people are seated around a large table. "Mr. Marks appreciates personality, and you have it in droves. It shows in your work, in your outfit…you're one of a kind."

This sounds like a pep talk my dad gave me before my first job.

I suspect Hugo is close in age to my father, so I take some comfort in his words of encouragement.

We round another corner with the heels of my boots clicking out a reminder of every step I'm taking toward the unknown.

"Good morning, Hugo." A dark-haired woman wearing a brown pantsuit approaches us. "I need to run up to marketing for a moment. He's expecting you. Go right on in."

"Thanks, Shirlene." Hugo smiles. "This is Juliet Bardin."

"Hi, Juliet." She raises a hand to wave at me.

"That's Mr. Marks's assistant," Hugo whispers as Shirlene walks toward a corridor. "That woman is the salt of the earth."

I nod, still taking in my surroundings while butterflies flutter in my stomach.

"This way." Hugo gestures to the right.

I make the turn and then stop as soon as I see the open double doors that reveal a gray-haired man sitting behind a desk that outshines the one in reception.

He pushes to his feet.

It's him.

Thurston Marks, the owner of Marks Creative, tosses me a broad smile, and with a clap of his hands, he calls out, "There she is. There's the woman we've been waiting for."

I WALK into Mr. Marks's office with Hugo on my heel. I have no idea if he's sticking around, but I secretly hope so.

Having a familiar face nearby would alleviate a lot of the anxiety that's taken hold of me.

Mr. Marks extends a hand as he rounds his desk. "It's good to meet you, Miss Bardin."

I shake his hand. "Please call me Juliet."

He nods but doesn't offer that same sentiment to me. Why would he? The man runs a media empire. I'm one of the thousands of people employed by him.

He buttons the jacket of his dark blue suit. "Juliet it is. I'd like you to meet Mr. Rothe."

I follow the path of his hand as it trails to the right. Another gray-haired man in a suit nods at me. He's wearing wire-rimmed glasses and has a phone in his hand.

When Hugo first hired me, I took an entire weekend to memorize the names of all of the executives at Marks Creative. I wanted to be prepared in case I ever ran into any of them in the elevator. Knowing someone's name before they are introduced to you can leave a lasting impression on them.

It can also be creepy as fuck but, so far, I've managed not to creep out anyone at Marks.

If Nigel Rothe works here, he has to be a new hire

because I don't recognize his name or face from any of the headshots on the Marks Creative website.

"It's good to meet you, Mr. Rothe." I move closer to him to shake his hand.

He offers me a smile along with the handshake. "The pleasure is mine, Miss Bardin."

"Juliet," I tell him as well.

"Why don't we all take a seat?" Mr. Marks motions toward three black leather chairs that are facing his desk. "We have a great deal to discuss."

I move first, claiming the middle chair as my own as Hugo sits to my right and Mr. Rothe to my left.

"We'll start with the non-disclosure agreement," Mr. Marks says, flipping open the cover of a file folder. "You'll sign this, Juliet."

Will I?

I know better than to sign something I haven't read.

He spins a piece of paper around to face me on the desk before he drops a silver pen on top of it. "It's a standard NDA. Hugo signed an identical one earlier."

I glance at it and then at Mr. Marks's smiling face. "I'll need a moment to look it over."

He looks at Hugo before his attention settles on me again. "Take all the time you need."

The document is short and sweet and outlines that I can't share any details about the meeting. That's it. There's no mention of the reason for the meeting. It's a standard NDA that essentially states that I'll keep my mouth shut about what's about to be said in this room.

I pick up the pen and sign it, knowing that all three men are watching my every move.

Mr. Marks slides the document back into the file folder, folds his hands together on his desk, and looks me dead in the eye. "You've been hand-picked for this assignment, Juliet."

Hugo decides now is the time to say something. "I'm not surprised. I think Juliet is the ideal person to interview Kavan Bane."

Kavan Bane?

Is that a real person or the name of a random guy-next-door movie character before he transforms into a superhero?

I swallow back the urge to ask that, and sit silently hoping someone will say something that will help me understand what the hell is happening right now.

"Mr. Bane has asked me to meet with you on his behalf." Nigel taps a finger against the armrest of the chair I'm sitting in.

"We all know the story that others want us to believe about him." Mr. Marks shakes his head.

No, we don't. Some of us don't have a clue about Kavan Bane's story or who he is.

"Juliet doesn't listen to the noise," Hugo says. "She respects the facts put in front of her. I'm confident that she'll handle this piece with tact and integrity."

Hugo looks to me for confirmation of that. I stare at him, blinking twice with the hope that he'll view it as a sign of distress.

Margot would since it's our secret way of communicating when we're with other people, and one of us feels uncomfortable.

Hugo smiles and gives me a hearty thumbs-up for good measure.

"You'll be compensated at the same rate as anyone else writing their first article for New York Viewpoint."

I turn to look at Mr. Marks, unsure if I heard him correctly. "New York Viewpoint?"

Straightening the already straight bow tie around his neck, he smiles. “Yes. Consider this your probationary assignment for a position as a lead journalist in that division.”

Feeling as though I’m in my bed dreaming this entire encounter, I reach down to pinch my thigh.

It hurts, so maybe, just maybe, this is reality?

“You’ll accompany me to my office now,” Nigel announces. “Naturally, we’ll have another NDA for you to sign. It will be more detailed, but you understand that.”

I don’t, but I’ll sign anything for the chance to land my dream job. I’ll read it over, but there’s a ninety-nine percent chance I’ll sign it.

Mr. Marks slides to his feet, as do the other two men, so I follow their lead, unsure if I can manage not to jump up and down in delight.

“Shirlene will be available to give you the grand tour of your new office anytime.” Mr. Marks smiles. “It’s a corner one. The views are brilliant. She’ll set up your expense account and handle anything else you need.”

“Thank you,” I say quietly, not sure what to add.

“Juliet will be working in an office that we provide for her for the duration of the assignment,” Nigel directs that to Mr. Marks.

The duration of the assignment? How long will it take me to write an article on this Bane person?

“Understood. If you have any questions or concerns, Nigel, you have my cell number.” Mr. Marks’s gaze drifts to me. “Shirlene will text you that number, Juliet.”

I nod.

He goes on, “I’m available for you night and day during this assignment. It’s an important one for us, so I expect you to make us proud.”

“I will, “ I say assuredly, even though I have no idea who

the man I'm interviewing is or what the scope of the article is supposed to cover.

Mr. Marks looks at Nigel. "We appreciate the fact that you came to us with this."

Nigel nods. "Mr. Bane insisted."

Mr. Bane seems like a guy who gets what he wants. I have no idea why he picked me for this assignment, but maybe he's a fan of my stellar work covering gossip for RumorMel.

I glance at Mr. Marks again. "Thank you, sir, for this opportunity. New York Viewpoint is my favorite magazine. I will give my all to this."

He leans forward. "I expect no less, Juliet. A lot is riding on your shoulders with this exclusive, but I trust you'll rise to the pressure."

I will. I need to. I've just been set on the fast track to my dream job, and I have no intention of failing. That's not an option.

CHAPTER TEN

JULIET

"YOUR PHONE, MISS BARDIN." Nigel holds out a palm as the driver of the SUV we got into pulls away from the curb.

I look to the left where he's seated beside me on the back seat. "What?"

"Your phone," he repeats without any context.

My hand dives into my purse to grab hold of my phone. I haven't looked at it since Hugo told me we were going to see Mr. Marks. After our meeting, he rode the elevator down to the lobby with Nigel and me.

He pulled me aside briefly to tell me that he was proud of me.

By the time that conversation was over, Nigel was instructing me to follow him to a black SUV idling next to the curb in front of the office tower that houses Marks Creative.

I got inside without question because I'm chasing my dream, and this is the path it's currently taking.

With my phone firmly in my grasp inside my purse, I stare blankly at Nigel.

"The moment your signature is on the required legal documents, I'll return your phone to you." His hand still bounces in the air, awaiting one of my most prized possessions.

It's also my lifeline in the event something goes horribly wrong. Why do I feel like I'm inching toward that right now?

"I'll turn it off," I offer in compromise.

"You'll watch me slide it into my pocket." His hand drops to pat the front of his suit jacket. "I will never leave your sight. It's strictly for security measures, Miss Bardin. Mr. Bane is a very private person."

"You're not going to take it and then drive me to a remote stretch of road to strangle me, are you?" I kind-of-but-not-really joke.

"I'm not driving," he deadpans before a smile slides over his lips. "You have my word that your phone will be in your hand as soon as we get the legal work out of the way."

I glance out the car's window. We're crawling through the early evening traffic in Manhattan. Since I already opened the window a crack, I know it wouldn't take me more than a second to inch it down more to call out for help.

There is no way that Mr. Marks would send me into a lion's den to fight for my life.

I try to quiet my overzealous imagination with a deep breath.

"We're almost there." Nigel's hand is back to its mid-air position. "The phone, please, Miss Bardin."

Against my better judgment, I tug it out of my purse and drop it in his hand, wishing I had taken two seconds before I got in this car to do a quick online search for Kavan Bane.

"Thank you," he responds as he slides my phone into the inner pocket of his suit jacket.

As the car pulls into a spot on Madison Avenue, I shove my hand into the pocket of my jacket. I take my keys in my hand and position them the way my father taught me to, so I'm ready for a jab, jab, slash if need be.

When my knuckles brush against the silk of the pocket square that I'm still carrying around with me, I close my eyes.

I survived an attempted mugging a block from here less than two weeks ago. Whatever I'm walking into now, I can live through too if I stay aware, keep my wits about me, and remember to check where every exit is.

MY FINGERS lessen their death grip on my keys as soon as we exit the SUV.

I look up – way up – as my gaze travels the height of the building we're about to enter.

It's a sleek silver column. It's taller than all of the other skyscrapers on this block, and architecturally it's a stunning work of art.

I look straight ahead to see the name of the building emblazoned in silver over the lobby doors.

Bane Enterprises.

I'm not up to speed on the big names in New York City business, but judging by the exterior of this building, Mr. Bane ranks high among them.

"This way, Juliet." Nigel motions for me to step into the lobby through one of the doors held open by a man in a crisp navy blue uniform, complete with a cap on his head trimmed in gold stitching.

"Good evening, Miss Bardin," he says in greeting.

That stops me mid-step. I turn to look him in the eye. "Good evening."

He offers me a smile and nothing more.

I'd ask how he knows my name, but I suspect Nigel is a stickler for details and a gentleman, so he warned the doormen that I'd be returning with him.

That was presumptive on his part, but no one in my position would turn down an assignment that results in a promotion that would otherwise take years to secure.

"We're headed to the right," Nigel instructs me. "There is a private elevator that will take us up to my office."

I nod in understanding as I fall in step beside him.

We avoid a few people rushing out of the building. I assume they are eager to start their weekends.

As soon as we approach an elevator tucked around a corner, a man standing next to it presses the call button. He's not dressed in the same uniform as the other two men who were holding open the lobby doors. This guy is dressed entirely in black.

"Welcome to Bane Enterprises, Miss Bardin," he offers with a smile as the doors to the elevator slide open in silence.

"Thank you," I whisper.

Drawing a deep breath, I board the lift knowing that this is the path to my future and I can handle whatever or whoever is waiting for me.

CHAPTER ELEVEN

KAVAN

SHE'S IN THE BUILDING.

I sensed it when I heard the ding of the private elevator announcing its arrival. That lured my gaze in the direction of the corridor outside my office.

I held my composure.

I didn't move to the doorway to watch Juliet walk past. I was tempted, which is why I turned my back to look out at the dusk-filled skies of this city.

The click of her heels on the marble floor was sure and steady.

If she's aware of what she's walking into, I admire her. If she's unaware, as I believe to be the case, she's brave beyond her appearance.

I was met with mild resistance when I called Thurston Marks earlier today and told him that I was available for an exclusive interview, but only if Juliet Bardin conducted it.

He threw the names of other people at me. They are experienced journalists who have masterfully handled politicians, business people, and celebrities alike.

I scoffed at each name before I reiterated my terms.

It was Juliet, or the interview would never happen.

He reluctantly agreed before we ended the call with the understanding that Nigel would attend the preliminary meeting with Juliet to inform her of her latest assignment.

Since she's here now, I assume that went well, and she agreed without question.

It's a step up from reporting on lost dogs and engagement rings.

The sharp jarring ring of my cell phone lures my attention to it.

I'd ignore it as I often do, but the name splayed across the screen is always an immediate answer for me.

I tap a finger on the screen to connect the call. "Locke."

"Bane," Graham says in an almost giddy tone. "It's Friday night, the stars are aligned, and I'm about to buy you a beer to end this week the right way."

"I don't drink beer," I remind him.

"I do," he replies with a chuckle. "You can order whatever the fuck you want if you're paying. If you expect me to pay, limit that shit to whatever costs less than ten bucks a glass."

Amused, I smile. "Later."

"Later as in tonight or later as in never, and you're about to hang up on me?"

"I'm in the middle of something." I drop into my office chair. That pulls a groan from the leather.

"I heard that." Graham's voice lowers. "Are you at the office?"

It's a fair question since I work at home most of the time. The whispered accusations that surround me whenever I am recognized have become a daily occurrence in my life that I've learned to live with.

However, I've come to realize that the people who work for me are far more productive when I'm not breathing down their necks.

I have no idea if fear grips them when they know I'm within arm's reach, but the bottom dollar is what matters most to me, and besides, my home office is far more comfortable than this one that my father spent a good part of the last twenty years of his life in.

I glance down at the desk. "I am."

"Why?" he spits that question out with a laugh. "You fucking hate that place."

Truer words have never been spoken. "It's a necessary burden sometimes, Locke."

Silence greets me in response until I hear him sigh. "What's going on?"

I glance up to find Nigel in the open doorway of my office. "I need to go."

"Meet me at nine," Graham says in a rush. "It's important, Bane."

"Make it eleven," I begrudgingly counter before I end the call.

With a curl of my fingers, I beckon Nigel into my office.

"Sir." He steps forward, scrubbing his hand over his forehead. "Miss Bardin has accepted the assignment. She's signing the required documentation now."

The documentation that prohibits her from discussing this project with anyone other than Thurston Marks, limits her ability to take pictures of me or anyone employed by me and guarantees that I get final say on her article before it's published.

"Was she resistant?"

Nigel sighs. “She requested a few minutes to look over the paperwork. I asked if she wanted me to bring in an outside attorney to go over the fine print with her, but she assured me that she has a grasp on the *legal jargon* we used. Her words not mine, sir.”

I don’t react even though I find her comment amusing. Everything she is required to sign is straightforward and necessary. There are no hidden clauses nestled within muddled language. It’s spelled out in the simplest of terms.

“I have a question if I may.” Nigel lets out a heavy exhale.

Leaning back in my office chair, I roll a hand in the air. “What is it?”

He steps closer to my desk and lowers his voice. “Why her?”

I perk a brow. “Explain that to me.”

“Sir,” he begins before he stops to shake his head. “I read some of her articles after you instructed me to attend the meeting with her and Mr. Marks.”

I nod. “And?”

“She hardly seems equipped to take on a task of this magnitude.”

Anger darts through me. I stop before I react because I don’t know where the hell that came from.

I don’t need to defend Juliet Bardin to anyone. I need to use her inexperience to my advantage, so I can put my past to rest and get this company back on solid financial ground.

“In my eyes, that makes her the ideal candidate.” I push to stand. “She’s not coming into this with a seasoned journalist’s perspective.”

Nigel nods. “She’s coming into this as a novice eager to get the byline. That means she’ll take the story she’s given. She won’t push for more.”

That's what I'm counting on.

"I'll check on the progress of the forms, sir."

"I want her in my office within the hour."

"Tonight?" Surprise edges his tone. "I thought we'd give her time for research before she's..."

"Her research begins now." I turn to look out at the skyline. "I'll be waiting for her, Nigel. Send her in alone."

"Very well, sir." His footsteps trail his words as he leaves my office.

CHAPTER TWELVE

JULIET

"I'M MEETING MR. BANE NOW?" I question Nigel as he scoops up the documents I just signed.

He glances at them before leveling his gaze on me. "Yes."

Dammit.

I thought we'd call it a night after this, and I'd be able to rush home to start researching Kavan Bane.

If pressed right now, I'd guess he's sporting just as much gray hair as Nigel and comes from old money.

Perhaps Mr. Bane wants to right a discretion by sitting down for an interview with me.

When I was reading over the documents Nigel left with me, my mind wandered to a few probable '*what if*' scenarios.

What if Mr. Bane is the sweet older man I sometimes buy a coffee for in the morning? That man is loaded. I can tell by the expensive watch on his wrist. He always thanks me with a smile, so maybe that goodwill gesture has finally paid off.

The other possibility is that my dad called a friend to help push my career into high gear. I asked him to promise me that he'd never use any of the connections he's made as a top-notch tax lawyer to aid me, but I wouldn't put it past him to contact someone he knows in New York City to ask for a favor.

He did something similar when Margot launched her lifestyle brand.

My dad reached out to almost everyone he knew and told them to do whatever they could to help my sister market the products she'd curated for her home decor collection.

Her business blew up within a few months. By the time she was celebrating her first year as the CEO of Arten Lorey, she'd passed her first million in revenue and had expanded her offerings to her own line of dishes, napkins, aprons, and anything else her clientele have requested of her.

"Mr. Bane is waiting," Nigel stresses each word.

I could ask for a momentary reprieve by pretending I need to use the washroom, but the curiosity of who orchestrated all of this is gnawing at me.

I suck in a deep breath. "I'm ready."

Nigel looks me over. "I can confirm that. You have nerves of steel, Juliet."

"I don't seem nervous to you?"

"Not at all." He shoves his glasses up the bridge of his nose with his fingertip. "Mr. Bane's office is this way."

I watch as his hand floats in the air with a finger pointing to the left down the corridor outside of his office.

"There is no time like the present, right?"

He nods. "Indeed."

We set off side-by-side in the direction he indicated. As we approach a set of closed frosted glass doors, I turn to him. "He's in there, isn't he?"

Nigel glances at me. "You're very astute."

I'm also foolish since I didn't bother glancing in that direction when I first arrived. I'd followed Nigel dutifully, keeping my gaze trained on his back because I was so deep in thought.

Nigel's hand dives into the inner pocket of his suit jacket. He tugs out my phone and offers it to me. "Here you go, Juliet."

I glance at the screen to see at least four notifications.

I should take a moment to look them over and to do a quick online search for Kavan Bane, but I catch sight of Nigel's hand reaching for the doorknob on one of the glass doors.

Dropping my phone into my purse, I take a deep breath. "I'm ready."

"The driver will be waiting for you in front of the building when you're done," he explains. "He will also be at your disposal during the course of your assignment."

"What's his name?"

"Drew," he says softly.

"All right."

Nigel turns the doorknob in his hand. "Go right in, Juliet. Godspeed."

My head snaps in his direction. "What?"

All he offers in response is a furrow of his brow. "Don't keep him waiting."

He pushes open the door an inch, and then scurries away leaving me standing in an empty hallway with a million reservations and one goal.

I'm going to write an article that will blow Mr. Marks away. There is no other option.

"Come in, Juliet," a man's deep voice calls from within the office I'm standing in front of.

Something stirs inside of me at the sound of that raspy tone.

It's vaguely familiar, and without another thought, I push open the door and take a step forward, feeling undeniably drawn to that voice.

I stop mid-step when I catch sight of his back.

The ends of his black hair fall over the collar of his suit jacket. The broad shoulders beneath it stop my heart for a full beat.

He turns to face me, and it feels as though time has slowed.

When his blue eyes lock on my face, I let out a small noise. It's nothing more than a whispered plea or a hushed moan.

It's him.

My savior, the man who rescued me from the clutches of a mugger two weeks ago, is standing in front of me with his arms crossed over his chest.

"Welcome to my world, Juliet," he says in a gruff tone. "I'm Kavan Bane."

CHAPTER THIRTEEN

KAVAN

REALIZATION SWEEPS over her expression like a soft wave before it crashes into the jagged edges of a rock.

Her hazel eyes widen. "You're Kavan Bane?"

Her reaction further cements my initial assumption. My name didn't come out of her full lips with anything more than surprise wrapped around it. There's no disdain attached to her voice. She doesn't view me as a man who stole something irreplaceable from this earth.

"I'm Kavan Bane," I say in a way that speaks my truth.

My mother suggested that I change my name after my father's death. Her reasoning was simple, or so she claimed. She told me that I'd be able to start anew somewhere far from New York City. In reality, she viewed that as her escape.

If I disappeared from the face of the earth, the stain that soiled her name and reputation would vanish too.

I never seriously entertained that idea.

I'm a Bane.

Regardless of what people associate that name with, it is a part of my father's legacy.

"Mr. Bane," she says my name softly.

I wait for more, but she stares at me, contemplating something.

"Juliet, come in." I gesture toward her. "Close the door behind you."

She turns to close the door softly before turning to face me.

She's dressed as casually as I'd expect, given the job I rescued her from. Thurston Marks rattled on about this assignment being her stepping-stone to a full-time position among the roster of journalists for New York Viewpoint.

It's not my concern where she lands professionally after this, although I suspect she'll have her choice of outlets desirous of her services.

I take a moment to admire the soft curve of her hips and the swell of her breasts beneath the floral dress she has on.

At another time, under different circumstances, I'd take her to bed.

That can't happen. I never mix anything with pleasure.

I fuck to fuck.

There are no romantic motivations behind that. I'm not looking for any entanglement. I want a release with a willing woman who is mature enough to realize that one-night stands serve a purpose.

"Come here," I say quietly. "Take a seat, Juliet."

She approaches me with steady steps before she settles into one of the chairs that face my desk.

I look down at her.

Her doe eyes are pinned to my face. Her lips are slightly parted.

For a brief moment, a sliver of regret slices through me because I can already tell that she would be a dream to fuck.

It's in the way she carries herself and her determination not to break eye contact with me.

That's a rarity for me.

"Why am I here?" she asks without so much as a blink of her eye.

"To write an article," I answer curtly.

"Why me?" she presses, adjusting her ass on the chair.

I watch as her legs cross, showing off a sliver of the smooth skin of her thigh.

My gaze trails back up to her face. I see strength and fortitude. But beneath that, there's a hint of confusion in the way her eyebrows have perked.

"You're a journalist," I state simply.

That lures a small smile to her lips. "That's not an answer to my question, Mr. Bane."

If I'm going to keep this professional, the Mr. Bane must stay.

Very few people call me Kavan, and I prefer it that way.

Her hand disappears into the pocket of the leather jacket she's wearing. She draws it out slowly with her fist wrapped around something.

"This belongs to you." She extends a hand to offer me a piece of fabric.

It takes a moment for me to realize what it is.

It's my pocket square.

I ignore the offering. "You had that with you today?"

Her hand drops to her lap. She opens it, smoothing a finger over the barely visible initials stitched into the fabric. The pocket square was a gift from someone years ago.

For anyone else, it might hold sentimental value, but for me, material possessions don't have a direct link to my heart.

Little does.

"I thought that if I ever saw you again, I could return it." She snatches it back into her fist and shoves it toward me. "I had it dry cleaned."

I reach for it.

The moment my hand brushes against hers, her breath catches. It's soft, barely audible, but it's enough to draw my eyes to her face.

I hold her gaze, wondering if that reaction came from the same electricity that pulsed through me when I felt her touch.

I take the pocket square from her.

Her gaze trails my movements. "Thank you again for helping me that night, Mr. Bane."

I nod. "I trust that Nigel explained the assignment to you."

"Not really," she says on a sigh. "All I've been told is that I'm writing an article about you."

I lean back to rest my ass against my desk. Buttoning my suit jacket, I study her face yet again. "Do you know who I am, Juliet?"

A brief look of panic dances in her eyes before she regains control of her emotions.

It's impressive and will be short-lived.

"You're Kavan Bane," she whispers. "You're the man in charge of Bane Enterprises."

Those puzzle pieces fell into place quickly based on my introduction and the name on the front of this building.

With both hands curled around the edge of my desk, I lean closer to her. "Correct, but there's more."

"More?" She swallows, luring my gaze to the elegant column of her neck.

"You're going to rush out of here tonight and research me, aren't you?"

"Yes," she admits. "I need to prepare for the assignment."

"The focus of your assignment is how I'm going to lead Bane Enterprises into the future," I explain.

Her ass edges forward on her chair. She's close enough now that I can smell the subtle fragrance of her perfume.

"I'll research the company," she says with confidence. "By Monday morning, I'll know Bane Enterprises inside and out."

That's commendable but unrealistic.

Any online search she conducts will yield thousands of results that have little to do with the inner workings of this organization.

"By the end of the day, you'll discover something about me." I stop to stare into her eyes. "Something that is completely off-limits when it comes to your assignment. You're not permitted to ask me any questions regarding it. I will never offer any details in relation to it. Is that clear?"

Curiosity lures her even closer to me. "What will I discover, Mr. Bane?"

I don't break our gaze as I say the words that once felt foreign to me but have now become as much a part of me as my skin and bones. "I killed my father five years ago."

CHAPTER FOURTEEN

JULIET

THE KEY to being a good journalist is to never let your emotions steal the focus of the job.

My favorite professor gave that piece of advice to me during my first semester in college.

It has stuck with me since.

I sit and absorb each of Mr. Bane's words.

If I break now, there is a very good chance I'll lose this assignment and any chance of securing a job with New York Viewpoint.

"That's off-limits," I state clearly. "Understood, Mr. Bane."

I can instantly tell that my reaction isn't what he anticipated. With narrowing eyes, his jaw tenses under his five o'clock shadow.

"You want the focus of the article to be on your business," I go on, convinced that my voice is coming out sounding strong and in control.

That's the opposite of how I feel inside.

All of the cloak and dagger stuff that preceded this meeting suddenly makes sense.

No phone, no pictures, no speaking of this assignment to anyone but Mr. Marks.

All of that was done to protect the man standing in front of me.

Surely, if he were guilty of the crime he just confessed to, he'd be serving a life sentence at Rikers.

I glance down at the skirt of my dress. Circling a fingertip around one of the pink roses in the patterned fabric, I take a breath before I look up and into his face again. "Do you have materials you think would be beneficial for me to go over? Anything that is relevant to the article I'll be writing?"

His arms cross his chest again. "I want to present a fresh perspective on Bane Enterprises, so I'd prefer if you garner all your information directly from me."

"We'll start on Monday?" I ask.

"Be ready for the driver at nine a.m. sharp, Juliet." He tilts his chin. "You can expect to put in a full day. I anticipate the process taking no more than a few days."

After that bombshell he dropped on me, I was hoping to wrap this up by lunchtime on Monday.

"I'll be ready." I stay seated because I sense I need to wait for him to lead us to the end of this meeting.

He studies me. "You moved to New York recently."

It's not a question, and I can't say that shocks me. He strikes me as the type of man who runs multiple background checks a day. He probably knows the entire life history of the tailor he buys his custom suits from.

"Six months ago."

"That's why you had no idea who I am."

It's egotistical to assume that everyone in the five

boroughs knows his name, but until I research the details surrounding his father's death, I won't know how sensational they are.

Maybe he's one of those trust fund kids who couldn't wait for the payout.

I'd guess he's a few years older than me.

He carries himself with the grace and confidence of a wealthy individual.

They're easy to spot in this city.

Honestly, he'd stand out in any crowd and not because of his pedigree.

"My only concern is your business, sir," I say in an even tone.

That lures the corners of his mouth up toward a smile, but it stops short of that. "That's all for tonight, Juliet."

That's my cue to get the hell out of here, so I stand.

"There will be someone waiting at the elevator to escort you to the car." He reaches to press a button on his desk phone.

I wait for the expected voice to ask what they can do for him, but instead I hear the ding of an elevator announcing its arrival in the distance.

His gaze trails up to meet mine again. "Goodnight, Juliet."

"Goodnight, Mr. Bane," I say before I slide the strap of my purse over my head and make a quick exit out of his office.

THIRTY MINUTES LATER, I'm at the bookstore around the corner from my apartment, still trying to catch my breath as I balance six thick books in my hand.

"Can I help?' A cute guy wearing dark-rimmed eyeglasses offers his hands to me. "I'll put these on the counter. When you're ready to check out, they'll be waiting for you."

I give him a better look. He's more than cute. His blonde hair is cut short. His green eyes are a shade lighter than freshly cut grass. "Do you work here?"

"I'm the owner." He motions for me to hand the books to him. "I'm Slate."

His name doesn't fit his image, but I kind of like that. I like his smile too.

"Juliet," I offer as I push the books at him.

"Such a beautiful name." He smiles before his gaze drops to the books. "It looks like you're a fan of true crime."

I'm not, but I'm a big fan of promotions, so I need to read up on who Kavan Bane is, even if none of that information can find its way into my article.

I have to understand the man if I'm going to present an article that is good enough to secure me the job I desperately want.

The online search I did in the SUV on my way home spelled out the crucial facts of the night Mr. Bane spoke of.

He was with his father, Ares Bane, in Miami when it happened. According to witnesses, there was arguing in the hotel suite that Kavan and his father were sharing, then a loud crash. Moments later, his father's body was discovered in the parking lot beneath a broken window in their suite.

Kavan was arrested within hours.

Just weeks before he was to stand trial, the charges were dropped.

The case drew so much media attention because Ares Bane was a philanthropist. The man funded many charities, built a reputation on his acts of goodwill and after his death, it was revealed that he was the anonymous donor behind not one but two children's hospitals along the eastern seaboard as well as a nationwide literary initiative.

I'm hopeful that the books I'm buying will give me more insight into Kavan and the company that his father founded decades before his death.

"You live in the neighborhood, don't you?" Slate asks.

Surprised that he knows that, I narrow my eyes. "Maybe."

He huffs out a deep-seated laugh. "I'm not stalking you. I've noticed you walking past."

With a tilt of his elbow, he motions toward the bank of windows at the front of the store. "I like to people watch. It's hard not to pay attention when you walk by."

I could get used to this level of flirting.

"I'll take these to the counter for you, Juliet," he says my name with a lilt at the end. "Maybe sometime when you're passing by, I'll stop you to say hi."

I smile. "Maybe I'd like that."

CHAPTER FIFTEEN

KAVAN

I SPOT Graham as soon as I enter the bar.

It's vacant except for him and the bartender. This is the very reason why I prefer to meet my friends for a drink here.

It's a small place close to my home that has a very limited clientele.

That's not by design but by fate.

The owner once complained to me that she was close to shutting down for good because sales had slipped once a few new bars popped up within blocks of here.

I pad her sales on a monthly basis to keep it open.

Perhaps if the entrance wasn't halfway down an alley, clear out of view of the street, she might be able to stay afloat on her own merit.

"Bane!" Graham calls to me from where he's seated next to the bar. "I'm over here."

That's typical Graham. Pointing out the obvious.

I stalk toward him. "Where are Sean and Harry?"

Normally, when Graham summons me to meet him for a drink, it quickly turns into a foursome.

"Not here." He laughs at his joke.

I shoot him a glance before I take the seat next to him.

There's no need for me to order. The whiskey I prefer will be set in front of me within seconds.

I nod when the bartender does just that.

I take a mouthful and swallow it quickly. "What's going on?"

"Let's start with why you were at the office today," he sidesteps the reason he called this meeting.

I shoot him a look meant to tell him to back off, but he's daydreaming about something because his eyes are pinned to the top of the bar.

"Let's not."

That lures his gaze in my direction. "You can handle anything from home except the board."

Nodding, I tap a finger against the rim of the tumbler in front of me. "It's related to the board."

"Are they still whining about revenue?" He shakes his head. "That will turn around. Tell them to fuck off."

"I have," I point out, before going on, "I prefer to do it in a way that won't cause them to revolt."

He takes a pull from the bottle of beer in his hand. "What do they want from you?"

"What they always want," I bite back. "Details, an apology, a time machine so I can redo that night and bring…"

"Ares back," he finishes my thought.

I take another mouthful of the amber liquid and let it trail down my throat slowly.

"They'll drop it at some point," he assures me. "It can't go on forever."

He's wrong about that. The board is acting at the behest

of the shareholders of Bane Enterprises. My father structured the company in such a way that he had to answer to them. I inherited his shares, so that burden falls on my shoulders.

"I've arranged to be interviewed beginning on Monday," I confess because soon it will be breaking news, and Graham, Sean, and Harrison deserve a heads-up.

"What?" This time the question is shrouded in disbelief.

I toss my head back and exhale. "It's not about that night. It's about my vision for the future growth of the company. This article is designed to shift the focus from the past to the future."

"You think that's going to work?"

"It will," I insist as I shoot a glance in his direction.

"What big name landed this interview?" he asks, concern edging his tone. "You're doing this in print, right? You're not going to appear on my TV screen."

"Print," I assure him. "The reporter's name is Juliet Bardin."

"Juliet Bardin?" he repeats. "Isn't that the woman who just nabbed the exclusive photos of Corla Berletti's engagement ring?"

A deep-seated chuckle escapes me. "How the fuck do you know that?"

He taps one of the pockets of his jeans. "Sean sent me the link."

"He's a Melster."

Graham's head falls back in laughter. "That's some funny shit, Bane."

I fight off a smile. "Juliet will interview me, and the article will appear in New York Viewpoint."

He pushes his dark hair back from his forehead. "She's going to push you about the past."

"She won't."

"She will," he argues. "Any journalist worth their weight will."

He's right, but Miss Bardin is too eager for the brass ring that has been dangled just out of her grasp. She wants a permanent job with New York Viewpoint, so she won't fuck this up.

Graham scratches his chin. "I hope to hell this goes the way you want it to, Kavan."

"It will." I sip from my glass. "Tell me why we're here, Locke. You didn't call me down here to probe me about my life."

He leans back. "You're right. I didn't."

I wait with a perked brow for him to say more, but he closes his eyes.

I give him a nudge with my elbow. "Spit it out, Graham. What do you need? Name it."

When his eyes pop open, I see something I've rarely seen before. Emotion has taken hold of my closest friend. The last time I witnessed this, he clumsily confessed to falling in love with his wife.

"What's going on?" I press. "Tell me."

His hand lands on my shoulder, and with a squeeze, he looks me dead in the eye. "I want you to be the godfather for my daughter, Bane. Trina and I are expecting a baby girl in six months."

I turn to the side to face him. "What the fuck?"

His hand doesn't move. "Trina insisted on waiting to tell anyone until she was past the first trimester. We talked about this, Kavan. Trina wants you to be the baby's godfather as much as I do."

I have no idea what the hell that entails, but I'd do anything for Graham and his wife.

"I'll do it."

He moves to embrace me. It's only happened a handful of times during our friendship. Most notably, the night I was released from jail.

Graham flew down to Miami to hire the best attorney in the state to represent me. Sean and Harrison trailed after him on the first flight the following morning.

Two days later, I was out on bail and headed back to New York City with a cloud hanging over my head that has yet to leave.

I give him a hearty pat on the back. "Congratulations, Locke."

Graham is on track toward the future he's always desired, and I've taken the first step to escape the past I've never wanted.

This is a night we'll both remember.

CHAPTER SIXTEEN

JULIET

I RUSH into the lobby of the building that houses Marks Creative's offices.

It's currently just past six p.m. on Saturday.

I was about to sit down for dinner with my sister at her favorite restaurant when I received a call from Mr. Marks.

My hands shook as I answered.

Margot was practically bouncing in her heels.

I haven't explained my newest assignment to her because legally I can't, and also, I don't want to worry her.

If I tell her that I'm going to be spending a few days next week interviewing one of the most notorious accused murderers in the country, she'll insist I take a job with her.

She's been trying to get me on staff for more than a year.

First, she wanted me to work as her assistant. That would have been an epic fail since I have zero experience in that capacity.

Her second offer was to write all the website copy for

Arten Lorey. I explained that my journalism degree didn't afford me the insight I would need to make gingham napkins sound irresistible to her clientele.

The pay and perks were tempting, but journalism is where I want to make my mark.

I jab a finger into the elevator call button three times.

Mr. Marks sounded serious during our call. He requested a meeting as soon as possible. He didn't need to tell me what it pertains to. I assume he wants an update on how my initial meeting with Kavan Bane went.

Fortunately, the NDA I signed at Mr. Bane's office allows me to speak to Mr. Marks about my article.

I jump onto the elevator the moment the doors slide open. Pushing a finger against the button for the top floor, I take a breath.

This is what I've always wanted, yet, after spending most of today reading a book titled *The Bad Bane*, I feel a knot of anxiety deep inside.

That book, written by a reporter based in Miami, portrays Kavan as a heartless killer with no regard for anyone.

That doesn't match with the man who saved me in the alley from the mugger.

That man showed compassion and concern.

He also said something to the mugger that convinced him to tell the police that I was the one who restrained him. I imagine Mr. Bane did that to keep his name out of it.

I understand why.

Even though the charges against him were dropped, he's still an accused murderer in everyone's eyes.

I have to wonder if that's who he is to me.

I shake off those thoughts and turn to look at one of the mirrored walls in the elevator car. I'm wearing an off-the-shoulder black and white fitted dress and a pair of red-soled heels my sister bought me last year. I don't consider this look professional, but there was no time for me to race home from the restaurant to change into something else.

Mr. Marks didn't summon me here for a fashion show. He brought me here because of the assignment he trusted me with. That assignment is about to change my life forever.

"THANK you for meeting with me on such short notice."

I glance across the desk at Mr. Marks. Apparently, Saturdays aren't casual days for him. He's dressed as he always is in a dark blue suit complete with a bowtie.

"Of course, sir."

He nods. "Were you able to meet with Mr. Bane last night?"

Crossing my legs, I lean back in the chair. "Yes, it was brief, but we met."

"Good," he says as he studies my face. "I'm wondering about something, Juliet."

"What's that?"

"What's your connection to Kavan Bane?" His eyes narrow. "There must be a reason why he chose you to handle this assignment."

I could confess that Kavan saved me from a mugger a few weeks ago, but I want Mr. Marks to focus on my talents as a journalist, not on some random encounter in an alley.

"He didn't say," I answer honestly.

Mr. Marks drums his fingers over the top of his desk. "When Mr. Rothe contacted me, he insisted that the article focus on the future of Bane Enterprises and Kavan's vision to turn the company around. I want to make my wishes clear to you, Juliet."

I perk up in my seat. My back goes ramrod straight. "What are your wishes, sir?"

He leans forward. "Kavan Bane killed his father five years ago, and every journalist in this country has been on the hunt for an exclusive with the man."

Tension grips my shoulders because I know where this discussion is headed.

Mr. Marks locks his eyes on mine. "I believe that you have the skill to shift the focus from Bane Enterprises to Kavan's story."

I hold up a hand in objection. "Sir, Mr. Bane made it very clear that the subject of his father's death is off-limits."

"You have been given an opportunity that people with decades more experience than you have been fighting for," he explains in an even tone. "It's your job to push the envelope, Juliet. Get him to open up. Convince him that this is his opportunity to set the record straight."

"I don't believe he wants to set the record straight."

"He does," he says with conviction as if he has access to Mr. Bane's private thoughts. "Anyone in that man's position would want that."

Feeling cornered, I struggle to find the right words. "Sir… Mr. Marks… I'm not sure that Mr. Bane will allow me to continue the interview process if I push him on anything personal. He was steadfast when he told me that the circumstances surrounding his father's death are off-limits."

"Juliet, this is your chance to prove that you are worthy of a senior position." He glances past me to the open door of his office.

Even though it's Saturday evening, many people are in the building, including on this floor. The news never stops.

"I understand that," I assure him.

"Keep this to yourself, but I've promoted Courtney

Cooper to a position with our London bureau. She'll make the move six weeks from now."

I try to hide the surprise that I'm feeling.

Courtney Cooper has been the face and voice of the morning news on Rise and Shine for more than two years. It's the most popular national morning news program.

"That's incredible for her," I say, wondering why he's telling me the new direction Courtney's career is taking.

"And for you," he whispers.

"For me?" I ask with skepticism. "How so?"

"If you nail this interview, Juliet, and get an exclusive on the night Ares Bane died, you are first in line to fill Courtney's chair when we start looking for a replacement."

This feels like a gift and a bribe all wrapped up in a not-so-tidy little bow.

I haven't even entertained the idea of an on-air position. In the furthest recesses of my mind, I briefly considered that it could be an option years from now after I'd put in my time researching hard-hitting topics.

"I want you to understand that if you don't nab an exclusive with Kavan about the night his father died, you will still have a position at Marks Creative."

Why do I feel as though that's his way of telling me that I may be knocked back down the ladder to RumorMel?

"I've been doing this for a very long time, Juliet." Mr. Marks smiles. "In my experience, when a person like Kavan Bane reaches out to the media, deep down they want to share their story. They may frame it one way, but with compassionate and careful guidance from the journalist, they just may see the light. After all, releasing a burden as heavy as the one he carries could very well change his life."

"And mine," I whisper.

"Exactly." His eyes shine. "Take it slow. Get to know the

man from the inside out. A lot can be gained by observing, and since you'll be by his side gathering research, I believe you'll deliver an article that we can all agree will benefit everyone."

An exclusive on the death of Ares Bane from the man accused of his murder will benefit Mr. Marks most of all. It will up his bottom line because he'll sell a hell of a lot of magazines in print and digitally.

"As I said yesterday, I'm available night and day for you, Juliet."

My gaze drifts to four framed pictures sitting on a shelf behind him. One is of him and his wife. I recognize her from the many searches of Mr. Marks that I did before I was interviewed for RumorMel.

The image next to that is of Mr. Marks and his son, Grayson. I know him from his award-winning poetry. Margot is a fan, so I gifted her a copy of his book for her birthday.

Another framed picture features a dark-haired man and a beautiful woman alongside two identical twin girls and an infant wrapped in a blue blanket. The last image is a woman who must be about my age. She's standing on a corner, holding a bouquet of roses while she smiles brightly at the camera.

"Family is everything, isn't it?"

My gaze trails to Mr. Mark's face. "Your family is lovely."

"They are," he agrees. "There is an image online of Kavan and his father taken just hours before his death on a beach in Miami."

I nod because I saw that photo online last night. I must have spent fifteen minutes staring at it.

Kavan's hair was shorter, and his blue eyes were hidden

behind a pair of designer sunglasses, but all the emotion he was feeling was visible.

He was smiling broadly with his arm wrapped around the shoulder of a man who stood a few inches shorter than him in the sand.

Ares Bane had the same black hair as his son and the same strong jawline.

With the ocean as their backdrop, the men stood side-by-side, obviously happy to be together, comfortable, content in a way that sometimes we can only be with our family members.

Less than five hours later, Ares was dead.

"There's a story there that is waiting to be told, Juliet." Mr. Marks glances at the framed photos of his family. "My gut never steers me wrong, and it's telling me that what happened in that hotel room in Miami needs to be shared with the world."

My gut is telling me that Kavan Bane would do anything to keep that story hidden forever.

"You're in a very enviable position," he goes on, "I know you recognize that and will do your best to take full advantage of it."

I read between those lines.

My boss wants me to dive deep into Mr. Bane's past even though I've been warned not to by the man himself.

Mr. Marks glances at his watch. "I'll give you a call in a few days to check on your progress, Juliet. If you need anything in the meantime, don't hesitate to ask."

I need to decide if pushing Mr. Bane is worth the risk.

The man controls my entire future, whether he knows it or not.

CHAPTER SEVENTEEN

KAVAN

MISTAKES THAT ARE REPEATED ARE OFTEN a source of regret.

I rarely venture into the overcrowded streets of Manhattan, but I did today to meet up with Sean.

I'm on my way home now, taking the route I often take, which is down alleys and up side streets.

Since my father's death there have been a few times when people who met him have spotted me. Sometimes all I'll get from them is a sneer. Other times they'll point a finger and call me a *bastard*, or a *waste of skin*, or the most common insult thrown my way is that I'm a *fucking murderer*.

Those words slide off of me. I've learned to ignore the rage in the faces of the people who approach me.

Often, if I move so much as an inch, they'll run in the opposite direction.

I have no idea if they think I'm going to wrap my hands

around their neck to squeeze the life out of them or if they worry that I'll defend myself with words.

I won't do either.

Others opinions of me stopped mattering the day my father died.

I quicken my pace to catch up with the woman who has decided it's a good idea to sprint down the same alley she was mugged in a few weeks ago.

Juliet Bardin, wearing a snug dress and black heels, is trying to make it past the scene of the crime untouched.

It takes me a few broad steps before I'm right behind her.

"Juliet," I say her name quietly enough that I hope to fuck it won't send her screaming in search of a savior.

That doesn't happen.

Instead, she stops abruptly and turns to face me.

Her cheeks are pink, her eyes rimmed with dark shadow and liner. She looks seductive, mesmerizing, and even more fuckable than she did last night in my office.

"Hi." She bites the corner of her bottom lip. "Hello, Mr. Bane."

"You enjoy tempting fate," I point out.

She laughs. "I'm prepared this time."

I glance down when she opens her fist to reveal a set of keys. The blade of one key is sticking out from between two of her fingers as if it's a weapon.

"I consider myself lucky that you didn't use that on me."

She sighs. "I recognized your voice. You have a very distinctive voice."

It's deep, some would claim there's always a threatening note to it, but I don't hear that.

"What are you doing in this part of the city?" I ask out of pure curiosity.

"Sneaking down alleys," she answers without pause.

I feel a twisted sense of satisfaction over the fact that she's not inching away from me. She's standing her ground, even though I'm confident that she's had enough time to read about the sordid details of the night my father died.

"There are safer routes to take to get where you're going, Juliet."

"I know." She looks into my eyes. "What's life without a little calculated risk?"

"Those are wise words from someone so young."

The lures another laugh from her, but this one is open-mouthed. "Someone so young? How old do you think I am?"

"You're twenty-five."

She nods. "You're twenty-nine."

"You've done some research."

Her gaze drifts to the right. "It's part of my job."

"Let me guess." I cross my arms over my chest. "You read some or all of *The Bad Bane*."

Her eyes travel over my shoulders to my biceps and then trail down the gray sweater I'm wearing to the front of my black pants before she looks at my face again. "I don't rely on fiction as a source for my articles."

"It's being marketed as true crime," I point out.

"True to who?" She drops one hand to her hip. "The author? You've never spoken to him, have you?"

"I haven't."

"The first rule of journalism is to rely on cold, hard facts." Her eyes never leave mine. "I prefer gathering information from the source than a third party who has no direct knowledge of the subject at hand."

This is a woman who takes her job seriously. That's not surprising given her inexperience and her eagerness to prove herself to Thurston Marks.

"Have you had dinner, Juliet?"

The abrupt subject change catches her off guard. I see a flash of confusion in her expression before she drops her gaze to the ground to find her bearings. “No. Not yet.”

“I live close.” I adjust the sleeve of my sweater to uncover my watch. “Join me there for dinner.”

She considers the invitation carefully, not saying anything as she searches my face for my motivation.

She won’t find it there.

Necessity has taught me how to shroud my emotions behind a blank expression. I’m inviting her home with me so I can set this interview process in motion as soon as possible.

It won’t go further than a few general questions about Bane Enterprises, but it’s an unexpected opportunity to lay the foundation of what I want the article to look like when we’re done.

“I can do that,” she says. “To talk about the article.”

“Of course.” I motion to the end of the alley leading out to Fifth Avenue. “This way, Juliet.”

She falls in step beside me, and even though the city around us is bursting with the noise generated by horns and the people who call this place home, I hear the faint sound of her keys hitting the bottom of her purse as they fall from her grip.

CHAPTER EIGHTEEN

JULIET

I WASN'T SURPRISED that a private elevator brought us up to Kavan's penthouse. An attendant was waiting at a side door of the skyscraper on Fifth Avenue. He let us in, and then we walked silently down a corridor to an elevator where a man greeted Mr. Bane by name.

He rode the elevator with us to the top floor of the building, and when we stepped off, he wished both of us a good night.

I thought I'd have a great night having dinner with my sister, but that fell to the wayside.

I'm currently standing in the foyer to Kavan Bane's penthouse while he has a hushed conversation with a man in a dark suit.

The man can't be much older than me. Behind them, a blonde-haired woman dressed in a chef's coat seems to be waiting her turn to get in the conversation.

I tear my gaze away from them to focus on the room in front of me.

It's an open space leading to a bank of windows opposite where I'm standing. Even from this distance, I can see the lit skyline of the city.

The décor is not what I expected, although I'm not sure what I thought I'd see when Kavan unlocked the door.

The floors are dark hardwood. The furniture is oversized and crafted in leather in masculine tones. There's a large rug near the fireplace. Next to that is an antique table and lamp. A stunning wooden cart sits nearby. Atop of it is an array of beautiful decanters; all are half-filled with amber liquids of varying shades.

The ambiance of the space is both strong and calming.

"Juliet." My name snaps off of Mr. Bane's lips. "Take a look at the menu for dinner."

A menu for dinner?

Judging by the chef's jacket draped around the woman standing next to Kavan, I assumed that she would be cooking for us.

I approach him and the woman. She can't be more than a few years older than me.

"Good evening, Miss Bardin," she greets me. "I'm Nara. I've prepared several options for dinner."

I glance down as her hand appears from her side with a piece of paper in it.

She shoves it at me, so I take it, glancing briefly at Mr. Bane.

I read it carefully.

There are two options for appetizers, three for entrees, and four for dessert.

"This seems like a lot of trouble," I say to her. "Whatever you were preparing for Mr. Bane is fine with me."

"Choose, Juliet." Kavan's voice comes out low.

My gaze trails up his chest to meet his eyes. I see power there and determination.

Nodding, I choose the first thing listed under each heading.

Lobster bisque.

Aged prime rib with seared mushrooms and a pan sauce.

Pears roasted in wine with honey ice cream.

I READ out each with a slight tremble in my voice before I hand the menu back to Nara.

She offers me a smile. "Excellent choices, Miss Bardin, and for the wine?"

I defer to Mr. Bane with a look.

Thankfully, he takes the hint and says the names of what I think are three different bottles of wine. The last is the only one I recognize. It's very expensive. I know that because I debated buying it to celebrate my sister's purchase of her apartment, but my budget wasn't on board.

Nara disappears around a corner.

I take a deep breath. "Your home is lovely."

He nods. "Take a seat, Juliet. I need to return a call. I'll be back shortly."

Grateful that I'll have a second to catch my breath, I set out toward a large couch set in the middle of the living room.

The color is a creamy light brown. A thin striped blanket is draped over the back.

In front of it there's a coffee table that features a large metal bowl filled with some decorative leaves and berries. Next to that is a perfectly fanned-out selection of finance and business magazines. Sitting on top is the most recent copy of New York Viewpoint.

As I take a seat, I stare at the cover.

That takes me right back to my earlier conversation with Mr. Marks.

No harm can come from considering his proposition. I'll go into this focused on Bane Enterprises, but if the opportunity presents itself, I'll take it and dive deeper into the night that Ares Bane died.

I steal a glance around the room to see beautiful artwork hanging from the walls, but there are no personal pictures. I don't see a framed photograph anywhere.

A soft sound behind me lures my gaze over my shoulder.

"Mr. Bane thought you might enjoy a pre-dinner drink." Nara extends a silver tray holding one glass garnished with a speared sour cherry. "It's a Manhattan. He said it was your favorite."

With a shaking hand, I take it from her. "It is, but how did he know?"

She smiles as his heavy footsteps approach from behind her.

"The articles you've written are a wealth of knowledge, Juliet," Kavan says, raising a tumbler partially filled with what looks like whiskey. "To the future."

I raise my glass too and whisper the same three words while I wonder exactly what the future has in store for me.

CHAPTER NINETEEN

KAVAN

TO GLANCE across my dining room table and see another face is rare.

I can count on one hand how many times I've had a guest here for dinner. Not one of those people has been as beautiful as Juliet.

With candlelight bathing her skin, she looks delicate, vulnerable, and surprisingly, she seems comfortable being in my home.

I was confident that when I saw her in the alley, she was on her way to meet someone for dinner.

I'm still convinced of that, but whoever it is, they've been given the brush-off.

"How long have you lived here?" she asks as she sets her fork down.

Dessert was served fifteen minutes ago.

We spent the first two courses talking about the city, the weather, and the falling crime rate.

It would seem that Juliet is a statistic nerd.

She recited the crime rate, including those related to burglaries and arsons in Manhattan for the past five years.

I listened even though the numbers meant nothing to me.

I've built a fortress here. My home is my sanctuary. Anyone wanting entry must make it past a doorman and the elevator attendant before they come face-to-face with Alcott when he answers the door. He's the son of the man who held the position before him.

My father saw the elder Alcott as his bodyguard. I view the younger Alcott, Birch Alcott, as more of a personal assistant.

He keeps things running smoothly in these ten thousand square feet of space. I not only live here, but this is where I do the bulk of my work.

Graham, Sean, and Harrison are permitted entry without having to jump through all those hoops, although I've instructed all six of the doormen to routinely give Graham a hard time when he shows up unannounced.

"A few years," I offer because that tidbit of information isn't relevant to the article she's researching.

She pushes her wavy brown hair over her bare shoulder. My gaze trails that.

"Do you like it?" She turns to look toward the bank of windows that border the dining area.

This penthouse affords me three hundred and sixty degree views of Manhattan. Each room offers a unique perspective of the city, although I have yet to discover one that can hold my attention longer than a few minutes.

Unlike now.

This view of Juliet is enthralling.

"It's adequate."

A small laugh escapes her. "Adequate? This is way above adequate."

I take a sip from the wine glass in front of me.

"Were you born in New York?" she continues on her quest to learn whatever she can about me.

I nod. "You weren't."

Her eyebrows perk. "You did your research, Mr. Bane."

"Denver, Colorado," I ignore her remark and instead point out where she was born. "You moved to California when you were ten."

"Ten and a half." She laughs. "The halves are important when you're that age."

I remember.

Every month was a milestone when I was a kid. Every accomplishment was another opportunity to make my father proud.

"Were you super intense when you were ten?"

I hold back a smile. "Am I super intense now?"

"On a scale of one to ten, you're an eleven."

"Not a twelve?"

A grin pulls at the corners of her lips. "I was being polite. You're more like a forty billion on that scale."

I tap a finger on the table. "I don't believe in coincidences, Juliet. You've read about my personal wealth."

She nods. "In Forbes."

"That article was written months ago," I point out.

She finishes the fruity dessert wine in her glass. "Is that your way of saying you're worth forty-one billion now?"

"More."

That lures a laugh from her. "What's an extra billion to a hot billionaire?"

Before I can respond, her hand is over her mouth.

"I meant… that's not… I didn't mean…" she stumbles through an excuse.

I lean back and give her the space she needs to find her composure. It's not the first time I've been referred to that way. It's the first time I've viewed it as a compliment.

"This ice cream is delicious." She runs a nail over the rim of the small dessert bowl that Nara served the ice cream in. "I need to ask Nara where she bought it. My sister loves ice cream."

There's a certain undeniable charm in the way she's trying to shift the conversation away from the fact that she finds me attractive.

"Nara made that."

Her mouth falls open. "You're joking?"

I can't recall a time in my life when I had a conversation quite like this with anyone other than my three friends.

People are on guard with me. It's that, or they are searching for something within my demeanor or hidden within my words.

"I'm not."

Her hand sweeps over her forehead, pushing back a few strands of her hair. "It's unbelievable. She should open an ice cream store."

I lean an elbow on the table and shift my position, so I'm slightly closer to her.

That movement is enough for me to see past the candle-light to the pinkish tone of her cheeks and the slightly glazed look in her eyes.

Juliet Bardin is drunk, or she's sipping her way toward that.

My father once told me that to truly understand a person, you had to keep their whiskey glass filled.

I've never viewed alcohol as a truth serum, but this is a rare opportunity for me to test the theory.

"My turn to ask a question, Juliet."

Her eyes widen. "Okay."

"Do I frighten you?"

She studies me, taking her time to respond. "Should I be frightened of you?"

I can't answer that question. A part of me wants her to be so she'll keep her distance, but there's another aspect to this.

There's an innocence to her that will make this process much easier for me.

I can guide her to write the article I want her to write.

She's eager to please Thurston Marks.

If we had met under different circumstances, I imagine she'd be eager to please me in ways that have nothing to do with her job.

I know, for sure, that'd I'd enjoy pleasing her.

Immensely.

The sound of soft footsteps lures her gaze over my shoulder. Her face brightens with a smile. "Nara! You are an incredible chef. You're awesomely phenomenal."

I don't turn to see the reaction on my private chef's face. I keep my eyes pinned to Juliet because she's breathtaking in a way that lights up a room.

I imagine beauty like hers could bring light to a man's life in immeasurable ways.

Perhaps it already is, and I stole a moment away from him tonight.

I push those thoughts aside.

Her personal life has no bearing on her journalistic skills.

Juliet is going to write an article that will shift the shareholders' and board members' focus back to where it belongs.

That's away from me and toward the business that my father entrusted me with.

"Thank you," Nara whispers as she clears our dishes. "Is there anything else I can get for either of you? Perhaps a brandy?"

The Manhattan and the three glasses of wine that followed are enough for Juliet.

I hold up a hand. "We're fine, Nara."

"Yes. We. Are. Fine," Juliet says with a flare of her eyes as she stares across the table at me.

Scrubbing the article and taking her to my bed is tempting, but that would complicate my life in a way I don't need right now.

I grip the edge of the table with both hands. "Tell Alcott to arrange for Drew to take Juliet home."

Nara mutters something in agreement before she walks away.

Juliet sighs. "The night has come to an end."

"It has." I push to stand before I round the table and place a hand on the back of her chair.

She looks up at me.

I stare into her eyes before my gaze drops. From this angle, the soft swell of the top of her breasts is visible.

"Dinner was nice," she whispers. "I'll see you on Monday, Mr. Bane."

I step back to give her room to stand. She does just that, finding her balance quickly before shifting to the right in her heels.

"Thank you again for this opportunity." Her eyes find mine. "I think it's going to change my life in a very big way."

It will. I have to wonder how much it's going to change mine.

CHAPTER TWENTY

JULIET

"DID you go on a bender last night?" My friend, Sinclair Morgan, asks as she slices a strawberry. "You could have skipped brunch for bed, Juliet."

Sinclair lives in the same building as I do.

When Margot and I moved in, Sinclair stopped by with a big basket of chocolate chip muffins. It didn't take us more than five minutes to realize that we both make our living as writers.

Sinclair does contract work as a ghostwriter. Her brother, Berk, owns a publishing company and has hired her to work on a few projects. Naturally, she hasn't been able to tell me what memoirs she's written, but it's made for a lot of fun every time I try and guess.

I tug on the waistband of the blue sweatpants I'm wearing. "I had a Manhattan and three glasses of wine."

Sinclair's head turns so abruptly that it sends her brown hair whipping over her shoulder. "Way to pound them back."

I rest a hand against my forehead. “I have such a bad headache.”

“You have a killer hangover,” she says as she breaks eggs into a glass bowl. “I knew it. I put a little something in your coffee that’ll help.”

I reach forward to scoop the ceramic mug from the coffee table. I give the contents a sniff, but all that greets me is the soothing scent of dark roasted beans. “It’s not a shot of something, is it? The last thing I need is more alcohol.”

“It’s a teaspoon of brown sugar,” she confesses. “My grandpa used to tell my brothers to drink that when they had too much beer.”

I take a small sip. I never put sugar in my coffee, but I may need to start. The sugar adds just the right note of sweetness.

Sinclair busies herself scrambling the eggs in a pan. “Were you on a date last night?”

One of the things we can talk about is the men in our lives. Currently, it’s the lack of men in our lives. We’re both casually dating and made a pact to never set each other up with anyone.

Bad set-ups can ruin friendships, and although I wouldn’t consider our friendship close, it’s fun, and having someone around my age to hang out with has been a plus.

Shaking my head, I take another sip of the coffee. “It was work.”

“Who were you trying to get a scoop on?” She chuckles. “The owner of a bar?”

Despite my best effort to avoid moving too much, my head falls back in laughter. “No.”

“I know you can’t tell me, but nod if you got drunk with a man.”

I nod.

"A good-looking, single man?"

I nod twice.

She glances down at the pan in front of her. "Was flirting involved?"

I wince. "I think I called him hot. It slipped out."

She points at me with a spatula in her hand. "What did he say when you called him hot?"

I look into the coffee cup. "Nothing. He skipped right on by that."

"Arrogant asshole," she spits out.

I laugh. "You have no idea, Sin."

She puts the eggs on two plates next to the strawberries and whole grain toast. "I will once the article pops up on RumorMel. I'll keep an eye out for it."

I wish I could tell her everything. I wanted to tell Margot too, but I can't. I'm legally bound to keep my mouth shut.

When the article is published in New York Viewpoint, I'll finally be able to bask in the glory of securing an interview with one of the most notorious men in the country.

"Let's eat," she approaches me with a plate in each hand. "Do you want to watch our favorite Duke?"

I reach for a plate of food even though I don't know how much of it I can stomach. "Absolutely."

Sinclair tucks her legs under her as she takes a seat next to me on her couch. Her blue eyes scan my face. "Maybe once this article is published, you and whoever you got drunk with can have some fun together."

"That's not going to happen."

She takes a bite of the corner of her toast. "You don't know that."

I reach forward to place my coffee mug back on the table. "He's intense, Sin. Crazy intense. This is an assignment, and once it's over, it's over."

Her gaze drops to the plate on her lap. "It's not over until fate says it is."

Fate.

That's a concept I used to believe in until fate proved that what it dishes out isn't always welcome.

WEARING a pair of charcoal gray pants, a short-sleeved white blouse, and my black heels, I step toward the SUV that I know Mr. Bane sent for me.

I recognize the driver, Drew, immediately.

He waves a hand as he pulls the vehicle next to the curb in front of my apartment building.

"That's your ride?" Ricky, the doorman, questions from behind me.

He asked if I needed help when I stepped off the elevator. I told him I was fine since the strap of my purse was wrapped around my body, courtesy of Margot. That did make it easier to carry my laptop case.

Nigel mentioned that I'd have an office to work in, but my own computer is a must.

I'm still considering what Mr. Marks said about the article. I know he wants me to dive deep into the night Ares Bane died. My plan is to test those waters to see how Kavan reacts.

After the other night, I'm more confident that I can push the envelope a bit without risking the assignment.

I glance over my shoulder. "It is."

Ricky smiles. "I hope you have a wonderful day, Juliet."

I offer him the expected, "*I hope you do too*," as Drew exits the car.

"Good morning, Miss Bardin," he greets me before

opening the back passenger door. "You'll find a cup of coffee there for you. Cream and sugar are on the center console. There is also a selection of pastries and fruit for you."

"Wow," Ricky whispers as he moves to stand next to me. "Someone is going all out to make your ride to work a special one."

I turn to look at him. "Don't mention this to Margot, okay?"

The last thing I need is my sister questioning me about the full-on buffet on wheels that swooped in to pick me up today.

"My lips are sealed, Juliet."

I guarantee that by handing him the twenty dollar bill that I tucked in the front pocket of my pants. I do that every morning, so I can stop and buy a large coffee and a pastry from Palla on Fifth.

They make the best cup of coffee in the city. It's pricey, but it's an investment that has always served me well. The extra jolt of caffeine keeps my energy level high for hours.

He thanks me with a curt nod of his head. "Let me help you with your laptop case."

Before I can hand it off to Ricky, Drew has it in his hands. "It's my pleasure to help in any way that I can, Miss Bardin."

With a shrug of my shoulders, I say goodbye to Ricky again and settle onto the soft leather of the back seat.

Scooping up the cup filled with coffee, I let out a sigh when I see the distinctive logo stamped on the side of it.

It's from Palla on Fifth.

Mr. Bane is either a mind reader, or the man knows almost everything there is to know about me.

CHAPTER TWENTY-ONE

JULIET

"I THOUGHT I'd be working at the Bane Enterprises building," I stress the last three words to Nigel.

He steps aside as a man with a briefcase rushes past us on the sidewalk.

"Mr. Bane prefers to work from home."

I look up at the building that houses Kavan's penthouse.

When I left here on Saturday night, I had no idea that less than thirty six hours later, I'd be back.

"We can conduct the interview at his office," I suggest. "Then I can work there piecing it together while he comes back here to work."

He shoots me a look. "That won't work. Mr. Bane is expecting you. I'll see you up and get you settled in your office."

"I have an office in his penthouse?"

He nods as if that's a normal thing. "I do as well."

I've heard stories about eccentric billionaires before, but this tops them all.

I understand that Mr. Bane has his reasons for wanting to stay out of the public eye, but this seems extreme.

I don't get to set the rules for this assignment, so I nod. "All right."

Nigel moves to grab my laptop case. "I can help with that."

I hold tightly to the handle, wanting to maintain control over something. "Thank you, but I'm fine."

He offers me a small smile. "I realize this may seem unorthodox, Juliet, but I assure you that you'll find your office comfortable."

"I'm sure I will," I say, even though I don't believe it because I didn't think I'd ever step foot in the penthouse again.

"Shall we head up?" I take one last long lingering look at the SUV that I just climbed out of.

It's my escape route. It's the way back to the normalcy of the life I had up until a few days ago.

It's also the direct route to either my desk in the RumorMel office or more likely, the unemployment line.

"I'm ready," I say with all the confidence I can muster as I head into the building where Kavan Bane is sitting in wait for me.

I GET the once-over as soon as I enter the penthouse.

Mr. Bane, dressed in a dark gray three-piece suit, black button-down shirt, and matching tie, rakes me from head-to-toe.

I look professional. My outfit won't win any awards for best-dressed journalist, but it's fine.

I'm here to gain insight into the stunning man in front of me. That's my only objective.

"I trust that the drive here was satisfactory."

It was in a luxury SUV with a free hot cup of coffee and delicious berries and grapes.

I usually take the subway to work, so this edges out that ten-fold.

"Yes, it was fine," I say because I don't want to focus on a car ride when there are much more important things to discuss.

"I have a conference call shortly." He glances at the big silver watch on his wrist.

It's an Abdons watch.

I know that because several of the celebrities I've chased after for stories have had similar watches.

"All right," I offer in response.

"Nigel will show you to your office." His hand motions to a corridor. "If you require anything, he'll help you."

I nod.

"We'll get started once my call is done." He glances at Nigel. "I need you back at the office by eleven to meet…"

"Understood," Nigel interrupts him in a rush as if Mr. Bane was about to reveal the name of someone notorious.

"Mrs. Baxter," Kavan finishes his thought.

That's a name I know, and there's nothing notorious about her. Beverly Baxter heads a charity that is focused on helping young pregnant women. Baxter House provides lodging and medical care. They also have many programs that support the moms and their children after birth and beyond.

In the limited research I've done on Bane Enterprises, I

haven't found a link between Baxter House and Bane Enterprises.

I make a mental note to question Kavan about that.

He studies my face. "I'll speak with you soon, Juliet."

I stand next to Nigel as I watch Kavan walk down a corridor and disappear into a doorway before the door softly closes.

"Are you ready to see your office?" There's a bright note in Nigel's voice.

I look up at him. "How long have you known him?"

I can tell he's debating whether or not he should answer the question. His eyes flit across my face before he looks down. "I was one of the first people to hold him after he was born."

As hard as that image is to render in my mind, I try.

"His life has been spotted with misery, Juliet." He lowers his voice. "He's come out of that with a level of strength that I admire."

Adjusting the strap of my purse over my chest, I nod. "You care about him."

He lets out a heavy exhale. "Like a son."

If a man as gentle as Nigel sees Kavan in that light, he can't be as bad as all the books I bought portray him to be.

"I trust him with my life," he adds. "There is no one else on earth that I can say that about."

I take in the slight smile on his face.

It suddenly disappears and is replaced with laughter. "Don't quote me on that, Juliet."

I laugh too. "Consider it off the record."

CHAPTER TWENTY-TWO

KAVAN

SCRUBBING A HAND OVER MY FOREHEAD, I slam my phone on my desk.

My father's connections in business are still haunting me.

He was the type of man who bought up companies that could barely stay afloat. With his magic touch, they'd blossom into something formidable. That always made the former owners proud.

Under my leadership, many of those same subsidiaries have breathed their last breath.

That's not a reflection of my business acumen. It's more about the ebb and flow of the economy and new trends that have taken over.

The conference call that just ended included two men who worked closely with my father for decades. They sought out those struggling businesses, made the introductions with my father and the owners, and took his direction when helping build them up.

Recently, I put both of them on notice.

They are well past the age of retirement, and it's time for them to move on and enjoy the trappings of the salaries and bonuses my father set them up with.

They are fighting me on that.

One went so far as to threaten to write a book detailing his knowledge of the months leading up to my father's death and the immediate aftermath of that.

I laughed in response.

I've lost count of the number of self-proclaimed insiders who have put pen to paper to write what they want to market as the '*shocking tell-all.*'

Since no one was in that hotel room in Miami but Ares and me, a tell-all will never hold the truth that I do inside of me.

A soft knock on my office door lures my gaze to it.

"Come in," I call out, wondering if it's Nigel, Juliet, or a member of my staff.

Nara and Alcott are here, as are a few other people I view as essential.

Drew is no doubt milling about, as is the woman who sees to it that my wardrobe is always in order, and my home.

As the door opens, Nigel appears. "I'm going to leave for the Baxter meeting, sir."

I move to stand. "Good."

"Juliet is in her office." A smile tugs at the corners of his lips. "She's comfortable there. It's obvious that she met Nara before today. They had a spirited discussion about honey ice cream."

I didn't see a need to fill Nigel in on my impromptu dinner party, but he's fishing for information now, so I satisfy his curiosity. "I crossed paths with Juliet on Saturday. She joined me for dinner."

"She did?"

Nigel doesn't do feigned surprise well. He had already pieced all of that together on his own.

"She's lovely, sir." He glances at me. "There is something refreshing about her."

I won't go down this path with him. Juliet Bardin is here for one reason and one reason only. She's going to write an article. Simple. When that task is complete, we'll part ways.

"The Baxter meeting, Nigel," I remind him with a tap of my finger against the face of my watch. "Don't keep Beverly waiting."

"Don't keep Juliet waiting," he counters. "She's eager to begin the interview."

I'm sure she is.

I'll take a moment to respond to a few emails, and then Juliet will be my only focus for the next few hours.

"YOU WANTED me to overhear Beverly Baxter's name," Juliet accuses as soon as I've sat down in a leather chair in the corner of the office I had set up for her.

It's a suitable space with a white table desk, a few flowering plants, and several pieces of framed art on the walls. All those are feminine and bright and will find their way into an auction benefitting Baxter House once Juliet's assignment is complete.

The artist is an up-and-comer that I've had my eye on for some time.

I cross my legs. "Did I?"

She tosses me a smirk from where she's seated in the white leather chair behind the desk. "Of course you did. You don't strike me as the type of man who lets anything slip."

Rubbing a hand over my chin, I nod. "Bane Enterprises has a long-standing relationship with Baxter House. You would have discovered that information on your own, Juliet."

She glances at the open laptop on the desk.

It's sitting next to the brand new, still boxed, one that Alcott ordered for her.

"I've spent over an hour trying to find a connection." Her gaze darts to the laptop screen. "Bane Enterprises isn't listed as a donor on the website for Baxter House, and there's no photographic evidence that you attended the fundraising gala they had a few months ago. You weren't at last year's event either."

I tap my fingers on my knee. "Photographic evidence?"

"Everyone at those events posts pictures online," she says. "Mrs. Baxter always hires a photographer to interact with the guests so she can use those images in future fundraising campaigns."

I'm not oblivious to how it works, but I'm enjoying her take on it.

Juliet has no idea that Bane Enterprises is Baxter House's biggest donor. That began after I took over. My father's generosity was always directed toward initiatives that made headlines.

I prefer to give without regard to appearances.

"I don't do galas." The word feels foreign coming from my lips.

"Your dad did." She taps a finger on the corner of her laptop screen. "I found an image of him and your mom at one. It was twenty years ago."

She throws that out as casually as someone would do when talking about the weather.

I ignore the comment. "You'd like to include the connection between Baxter House and Bane Enterprises in your article."

"You'd like that too," she says pointedly. "That's why you dropped her name on me in the foyer."

She's perceptive.

"What other charities are benefitting from your generosity, Mr. Bane?"

"You're assuming there are more, Juliet."

"It's not an assumption." She leans back in her chair. "On the table in the foyer, there's an envelope addressed to you from The Foster Foundation."

If there is, that wasn't by design.

Alcott must have dropped the mail he picked up at Bane Enterprises this morning on that table before he went to tend to another task.

On a typical day, Nigel rifles through it to pick out whatever needs my attention. The rest would be directed to my lawyer, accountant, or whoever is best equipped to deal with it.

"The Foster Foundation helps people who can't afford medical care," she recites the organization's mission almost word-for-word. "You donate to them as well, don't you?"

"Bane Enterprises does," I clarify since the focus of her article is on my company, not me.

That sets her forward in her seat. "Do you fund any charitable causes, Mr. Bane?"

Many, but we aren't going there.

I intend to keep my personal finances private.

"I take it the non-answer is a yes?" She smiles.

"You should take it at face value, Juliet." I keep my expression stoic. "A non-answer is just that. It's not an answer. Don't assume anything."

Her hazel eyes trail over my face. “It’s too late for that, Kavan. I’ve already made some assumptions about you.”

Kavan.

I’ve never heard my name sound quite like that.

“It’s okay for me to call you that, right?” A smile slides over her full lips. “We are going to be spending a lot of time together while I learn more about you.”

“About the business,” I correct her, but I don’t take it further.

Very few people call me by my first name, but I won’t stop her if she wants to.

“Right.” She nods. “This is all about the business.”

CHAPTER TWENTY-THREE

JULIET

I THOUGHT Kavan Bane in a three-piece suit was a treat for the eyes. Seeing him without the jacket, in just the vest, with the ends of his dark hair brushing his shirt collar, quickens the beats of my heart.

He looks like one of the devilish Rakes on the show that I can't seem to get enough of.

He's standing in the doorway of my office, glaring at me.

If this has to do with the fact that I called him Kavan instead of Mr. Bane, he can spank me.

I hold in a laugh and maybe even a tiny moan while I think about that.

He's the type of man who must fuck a woman senseless. He probably leaves women in such an orgasm-fueled trance that they can't remember their own names.

I've never had an experience like that.

I can't recall most of the names of the handful of men

I've slept with in the past. Regrettably, they are all that forgettable.

"Juliet," my name snaps off his lips. "I just spoke to Nara."

I know where this is going.

It seems that Nara is required to plan a three-course menu for every meal. She's been doing that almost daily for two years. She explained that to me when she presented today's lunch menu to me when Kavan stepped out of my office to take a call.

I told her to prepare whatever inspired her for lunch.

I'm guessing that wasn't the right choice.

I rest both elbows on my desk. "It's about lunch, right?"

Leaning one of his biceps against the doorjamb, he crosses his arms over his chest.

He has the whole bad boy/boss man vibe down pat.

There's a lot more to him than meets the eye. He's thoughtful, even if he'd never admit it. When I mentioned his parents, I saw the subtle shift in his expression.

He may have thought he was being stoic, but sadness seeped into his eyes before he tore his gaze away from me.

"You didn't choose."

I nod. "I like surprises."

He doesn't say a word, but I swear I spot a ghost of a grin on his mouth. "Did you smile?"

His lips fall into a straight line. "No."

I push up to my feet. "You did."

"Juliet." My name comes out with a bite of frustration attached to it. "Choose what you want for lunch."

"Nara is going to choose."

"I want you to choose."

Unable to comprehend why this matters so much, I stand

my ground because I don't think he deals with that often, if at all.

I've learned that the best way to defend yourself is to own your actions, thoughts, and beliefs.

Right now, I believe that Nara will prepare something worthy of a five-star restaurant for lunch.

I'd be happy with a PB and J sandwich, but I don't think Kavan knows what that tastes like.

"Why does it matter?" I smooth a hand over the front of my blouse, my fingers scattering up the row of pearl buttons.

His gaze follows that path until it rests on my breasts before he looks me in the eye.

Staring into his intense blue eyes, I suddenly realize what this is all about.

It's control.

He's giving up one small slice of control to me. He's handing it to me as a gift, even if he's not fully aware that's what he's doing.

"I'll go talk to Nara," I say as I round the desk. "I'll choose the lunch menu, Kavan."

He stands stoic in my path in the doorway.

I look up to meet his gaze with mine.

His jaw is less tensed, his brow not furrowed anymore. "Good."

"After lunch, we'll get back to the interview?" I ask.

"Drew will take you home after lunch. I have meetings all afternoon."

"But," I begin to argue that at this rate, it will take me months to finish the article. I stop myself, though, because a snail's pace may just be what I need to dive into the innermost corners of Mr. Bane's mind and his heart so I can deliver the article worthy of a byline in New York Viewpoint.

"But?" he repeats softly.

"But, I'd prefer to walk," I blurt out as an excuse. "I need to run a few errands."

His hand moves toward my chin, but he pulls it back abruptly. "Stay out of alleys, Juliet. I won't be there to save you."

I tilt my chin up as a beacon, but his hand falls to his side. "I can save myself."

"I'm sure you can," he says before he steps to the side to give me room to pass by.

I HAD no idea lunch would be a threesome.

Nigel appeared at the table just as I was about to take a seat. I hadn't heard him come back to the penthouse, but that's likely because I was tucked away in my office, searching Google for anything it could tell me about Kavan Bane.

The man himself went back into his office after I told him I'd choose the menu.

Now, we're seated at the dining room table, eating bowls of spiced carrot soup as an appetizer.

There are Brie and fig salads to come and fresh fruit tarts.

I'll be skipping dinner tonight.

"What made you want to pursue a career in journalism, Juliet?"

I look toward Nigel since he asked the question. "I crave information. I find people fascinating."

Nigel's gaze doesn't falter. "My mother was a journalist."

"For a magazine?" I ask.

"Newspaper," he answers swiftly. "She started as a reporter but worked her way up to senior editor."

"Impressive." I toss him a smile. "Did you ever think about following in her footsteps?"

"Me?" he says with an exaggerated poke in his chest with his finger. "That's not my forte."

When Nara arrives with three plates heavily loaded with fresh salad greens, figs, cheese, and a delicious smelling dressing, the conversation stalls.

I thank her, as does Nigel, when she clears the soup bowls.

I slide my fork around my plate, tugging on a piece of lettuce with the tines. "What is your forte, Nigel? Besides, your job with Bane Enterprises."

He sets his fork down. "I'm not sure I follow, Juliet."

I steal a glance at Kavan to find him watching the two of us in silence. Redirecting my attention back to Nigel, I tap the top of his hand with mine. "When you're not working at Bane, what do you like to do? What are you really good at?"

His cheeks flood with pink. "It's embarrassing."

"Tell me." I lower my voice. "If I had to guess, I think it must be related to birds."

That's enough to bring a smile back to his face. "I bird watch in Central Park."

"You do?" Kavan's voice breaks into our conversation.

Nigel looks at him. "As often as my schedule allows."

"That's fascinating." I lean back in my chair. "Are there many different birds to see there?"

"So many." His face lights up. "I sort them all by color. I have an entire binder filled with pictures, dates, facts…all of it is there."

Kavan watches Nigel carefully. I can tell that he had no idea that his right-hand man was a birdwatcher.

Nigel reaches to squeeze my hand. "How did you know it was related to birds, Juliet? I haven't mentioned it to you."

I tilt my chin to the right. "The day we met you were wearing a peacock pin on your lapel. Today, it's a robin."

His gaze drops to the pin, as does Kavan's.

Nigel pats his hand over the pin. "They belonged to my wife. When she died, I promised her I'd keep bird watching for the both of us. It helps me feel as though she's still with me."

I reach forward to straighten the pin for him. "I think that bird watching is definitely your forte."

With tears welling in his eyes, he nods. "I'd agree."

I look toward Kavan to find his gaze locked on the robin pin.

He's been living in a hell of his own making for so long that he didn't see that the man who views him as a son was trying to create his own slice of heaven on earth.

CHAPTER TWENTY-FOUR

JULIET

I ASKED Drew to drop me off three blocks from my apartment, so I could walk off at least a few of the calories I consumed at lunch.

As an extra special treat just for me, Nara added a small bowl of honey ice cream next to my fruit tart.

Once lunch was over and Kavan went back into his office to take care of more calls, I hugged the chef.

She was taken aback, but she returned the hug and thanked me for thanking her.

Kavan Bane may be hot-as-fuck, but he's also apparently rude-as-hell.

It doesn't hurt to thank people who help you, whether you're paying them or not.

I spot my destination a half of a block ahead.

I'm going to stop in the bookstore and have a quick peek at the new memoirs released today.

It's fuel for my next guessing game with Sinclair.

She'll get a kick out of it, and I'll get to spend more time with her.

I wave to the woman who runs a small bistro that I often stop at for brunch with Margot. She's outside, writing something on the sign that faces the sidewalk traffic.

I stop to take a read.

"A jellied, plum torte?" I sigh. "Yes, please."

"You want one?" she questions with a grin.

"Margot will love it."

"I can attest to that," she says as she leads me into the bistro. "Your sister stopped by for a taste test last week."

Curiosity piqued, I tap her shoulder. "With or without a man?"

She laughs. "Without. I have a son around her age. He's smart, successful, and handsome. That checks all Margot's boxes, right?"

I watch as she slides a decadent looking torte from the display case. "It does but Margot will tell you that she's too busy with work for love."

Carrying the torte across the bistro toward a stack of pink boxes, she shakes her head. "No one is too busy for love."

I won't argue with her.

I glance around at all the offerings. "What can I take home for Margot for dinner? Something light."

"The broccoli quiche will put a smile on her face." She starts toward another display case. "I'll pack all of this up for you, Juliet. Your sister will be pleased as punch once she gets home from work."

If she gets home from work before I go to bed.

Margot puts in long hours, but it's her joy, so I've never tried to get her to change.

"JULIET!" The dulcet tones of a man's voice pull at me from the left.

I dart my gaze over the crowded sidewalk trying to find a recognizable face that I can attach to that voice.

I come up empty.

"Over here, Juliet."

This time I spot the owner of the voice immediately. It's Slate.

That makes sense, given that I'm just feet away from the door to his store.

He's standing in the doorway, with a muscular arm raised in the air in greeting.

I'm not the only woman who has turned to look.

I make my way toward him, holding tightly to the strings of the stacked boxes I got from the bistro in one hand. My laptop bag's handle is firmly within the grasp of my other hand.

"Hey, Slate," I say as soon as I'm close enough that I know he'll hear me.

"Are you coming in?" he asks, adjusting the frame of his glasses.

My gaze drops to the gray T-shirt he's wearing. It bears the name of a college hockey team. I've never asked how old he is, but if pressed to guess, I think he must be my age or a year or two older.

"My alma mater," he says as he tugs on the front of his shirt.

That sends the bottom hem up a few inches to reveal a toned stomach complete with a trail of dark hair.

I tear my gaze away from that and focus on his face. "I thought I could spend a few minutes browsing the memoir section."

He nods. "Are you looking for anything in particular?"

I decide to take a shortcut that I haven't before. "Anything published by Morgan Press."

The corners of his lips quirk. "I've got a few of those on hand."

Stepping into the shop, I smile. "Great. Point me in that direction."

"Why don't I guard those bistro goodies, so you have a free hand?" He reaches out to me. "It looks like you're all set for dinner tonight."

I nod.

Taking the boxes from me, he glances in my direction. "What about tomorrow night? Do you have dinner plans?"

This is unexpected but not unwelcome.

I haven't been on a date in weeks, and he's cute. He's friendly too.

"I don't," I answer quietly.

"Have dinner with me," he pauses, "I mean do you want to have dinner with me?"

Margot once told me not to seem too eager, so I take a second before answering.

That's apparently too long for Slate because he clears his throat. "I'm not suggesting anything fancy. Let's do informal. Jeans, burgers, maybe a beer."

The jeans and burgers work for me, but I can't stomach the taste of beer. "I'd like that a lot."

"Great." He grins. "I close up at eight. I can walk over to your building to pick you up, or…"

"I'll walk over here," I suggest.

"It's a date." He looks into my eyes. "I'm looking forward to this, Juliet."

"I am too," I say honestly.

I deserve to have some fun, especially since I'll be spending at least part of my day with moody Mr. Bane.

CHAPTER TWENTY-FIVE

KAVAN

"IS THERE anything else you need before I leave, Mr. Bane?"

I turn to see Nigel standing in the doorway of my office. It's nearing seven. I had a busy afternoon of meetings via phone. Nigel sat in for some, and during others, he tended to work I had assigned him.

I beckon him into my office with a curl of my fingers. "Come and sit."

He doesn't hesitate.

Nigel never hesitates when I ask anything of him, even when it is unthinkable, as it was the night my father died.

Nigel rushed into the hotel room moments after my father took his last breath.

I was the calm one. Nigel was panicked, but he followed my directions, never questioning the *whys*. He just did what I asked. I'm sure back then, his loyalty was born from his bond with my father, but we've found a rhythm that works for us, or I thought we had.

After Nigel's discussion with Juliet at lunch, I'm beginning to wonder how well I know him.

Once he's seated in front of my desk, I cross my arms. "Did Ares know about the bird watching?"

Uncertainty stills his expression. His eyes widen. That's a sure sign that Nigel's having an internal debate.

I've seen it before, dozens of times, but that's always been during a discussion about business.

"He introduced us to it."

I stare at his face as those words sink in. "My father introduced you to bird watching?"

"He sent Golda and me on a honeymoon to Peru." His gaze falls to his lap. "There was a park there that he had visited as a child. He bird watched with his own father during that trip."

It's almost too much to process at once.

Imagining my father in a park with a pair of binoculars strung around his neck is an image so outrageous that I can't conjure it up.

"Back then, before you were born, he often spoke about how he'd take his children to that same park."

That's a blow because the only trips I took with my father were to destinations where he could expand his business holdings. That included jaunts to Europe, Australia, and cities all over the United States, including Miami on that fateful night.

"His business grew," Nigel continues. "Personal trips fell to the wayside."

Scrubbing a hand over the back of my neck, I let out a heavy exhale. "I didn't know."

"Ares was a different man after he found success." His tone drops. "I often wished that things were…"

When his voice trails, I don't push for more. My mother had echoed those same sentiments for years before my father died.

We sit in silence for a moment.

"Juliet is charming." He taps a finger in the air. "Smart, insightful, and there's her smile."

There's much more to her than that but I don't go there, because Juliet Bardin is in my life for only one reason.

"Did you start the interview process today, sir?"

"She asked a few questions. I answered."

"That is how interviews work." He laughs.

Stoic, I look behind him to the doorway. Soon, I'll choose a dinner menu that Nara will prepare.

I'm tempted to ask Nigel to join me, but I'll be more comfortable with my own company tonight.

Today was jarring. It was unexpected.

Juliet Bardin has spun into my life like a whirlwind.

I need to find my bearings so that tomorrow, I can face the day with a clearer mind and focused intent to keep Juliet on topic.

"I BROUGHT PASTRIES FOR EVERYONE," Juliet announces as she parades into the foyer of my penthouse dressed in white pants, a sheer black blouse, and red heels.

Jesus.

It's a look that suits her, although the woman herself is stunning. An article of clothing doesn't exist that could add anything to her beauty.

A sudden vision of what she must look like nude flashes through my mind.

I chase that away with a hard swallow.

"Do any of them have lemon filling?" Nigel asks as he peers into the now open pastry box.

"Of course." Juliet glances at him. "Alcott told me lemon curd is your jam."

Nigel tosses his head back in laughter. "I see what you did there. I prefer lemon curd on my toast as opposed to jam."

What in the actual fuck is going on?

This is my home. It's where I conduct business. It's not a goddamn staff room where people can exchange recipes and sample each other's pastries.

I have no idea if that is a thing, but Juliet Bardin is upending my routine in a way that I don't want.

"Juliet," I bark out her name.

That spins her around to face me. The black satin bra under her blouse is doing little to conceal the outline of her hardened nipples.

She pushes a strand of her hair back from her cheek. "Yes?"

I fist my hands at my sides in a desperate attempt to control what feels like need.

What the fuck do I need right now?

Peace and solace or her in my bed beneath me, taking each deep thrust of my…

"Mr. Bane would like to get started with the interview immediately," Nigel lies. "It would be preferable if we wrapped it up for the day before six."

I turn to him and silently quiz him with a lift of one eyebrow.

"I have dinner plans, sir," he explains. "An old friend is in town."

"I have dinner plans too," Juliet chimes in. "With a new friend."

That piques my interest enough that I momentarily forget that I'm pissed with the pastry escapades.

"Am I right to assume it's with a gentleman?" Nigel asks.

"Slate," she says quickly. "His name is Slate."

"That's edgy." Nigel smiles at her. "You mentioned that he's a new friend. Is this the all-important first date?"

Keeping her gaze trained on Nigel's face, she nods. "We're going to keep it casual. Jeans, T-shirts, maybe a burger, and then we'll see where the night takes us."

"Slate is a very lucky man." Nigel shoots me a look, but I ignore him.

"We need to get started, Juliet." I summon her with a curl of my finger.

She starts on her approach with the pastry box still in her hands.

I tilt my chin up. "Leave those on the table."

She does just that but steals something soft and fluffy from the box before she turns to face me again. She takes a bite of it, and that's immediately followed by a slow lick of her tongue over her bottom lip.

It's carnal in a way I'm not expecting. The need it feeds within me is so fierce that I want to stalk toward her, grab her, and tug that plump lip between my teeth.

"I'm ready," she announces before she takes a second bite.

I turn my back, not sure if I can handle another stroke of her tongue over her lip.

I'm hard from watching her eat.

I close my eyes, rub a hand over my forehead, and start in the direction of her office, hoping that by the time I face her again, my cock will have calmed the hell down.

CHAPTER TWENTY-SIX

JULIET

"WE'RE GOING to continue this tonight, Juliet."

Since he's not looking at me, I roll my eyes.

Why did I think *that* was going to happen?

Kavan Bane is clearly a man who demands attention and sucks all the fun out of the room with one big gulp.

I saw it this morning when I brought pastries for the staff.

I thought Nara deserved a treat since she works her fingers to the bone trying to please a man who didn't even finish his sandwich at lunch today.

Who doesn't eat all of a sandwich that contains prosciutto?

Lunch was my choice again.

I opted for the sandwich, a crostini slathered in roasted tomato puree for the appetizer, and then I insisted that we dine on the pastries I brought for dessert.

Bane marched out of the room then.

I watched him leave, admiring the cut of his shirt and the

way his ass looked in his pants. He had ditched the suit jacket again this morning after I questioned him about a subsidiary of Bane Enterprises that is facing legal action.

I dug that little nugget out of a lawsuit registry in Arizona.

I thought if I threw something negative at him, he'd volley with something positive.

That was an epic fail.

He spent the better part of an hour schooling me on the legal reach of a suit like that and how it doesn't impact Bane Enterprises' bottom line in the least.

I listened intently while staring at him because he really is *that* good-looking, especially unshaven.

"I have a date," I say because I have no idea if he was paying attention when I was spilling the details to Nigel this morning in the foyer.

"Is it as important as this?"

Um...yes.

I keep that to myself and smile. "I think we should regroup and start fresh in the morning."

It's a solid statement, considering the fact that I spent much of today waiting to speak to him.

He sliced out that hour this morning for my law lesson and then almost an hour at lunch before he staged the pastry protest and stomped out of the room.

The only other time I spoke to him was a brief fifteen minutes late this afternoon when he caught me flipping through the magazines on his coffee table.

Unsurprisingly, they all featured articles that mentioned Bane Enterprises.

Not one of them contained information that isn't readily available online.

I was sure that he'd dismiss me early again today, but that didn't happen.

It's now nearing seven, and I was hoping to head home to change into something less sheer for my first date with Slate.

"I think we should have dinner together and discuss the future of Bane Enterprises."

I search for a comeback, but before I can pull something out of the blue, his phone rings.

I close my eyes briefly, praying that it's a business catastrophe that demands his immediate attention. The plus to that is tomorrow he can fill me in on the details so I can add it to my article.

"Harrison," he bites out as he answers the phone.

His gaze runs over my face as he listens to whoever is on the other end of the call.

"Tonight?" he asks with a heavy sigh. "You're sure it has to be tonight, Harry?"

I silently thank Harry (whoever he is) for whatever he's currently saying to Kavan because it sounds like my almost canceled date is back on.

"I'll meet you at Sérénité in thirty minutes." He lowers his voice. "The private dining room."

I watch as he turns his back to me. "It'll be all right, Harry."

Reassurance coming from the lips of Kavan Bane?

Maybe I should ditch my date and book a table at Sérénité for a good old-fashioned journalist seek and find mission.

I'll seek out this Harry person and find out why Bane is nice to him.

The problem is that Sérénité is a fancy French restaurant on Tenth Avenue with no reservations for the next six months.

Margot tried to book us a table there last month. The host

who answered the call practically laughed at her when she said she wanted a table for two that night.

Kavan ends the call without so much as a '*goodbye*' or '*see you soon, Harry*'.

When he turns back to face me, the stoic expression is back on his face. "We'll have to continue this tomorrow, Juliet."

"We will," I assure him with a nod of my chin.

He turns on his heel. "Alcott will arrange for Drew to take you home."

"I hope everything is okay," I say quietly.

That spins him back around. "What was that?"

I look down before I settle my gaze on his face. "I hope that whoever Harry is, that he's all right."

He takes measured steps toward me until the toes of his shoes almost brush against mine. "That call wasn't your concern, Juliet."

I tilt my chin up. "I didn't say it was, Kavan. I couldn't help but overhear, and it sounded as though the person you were speaking to needed you. All I said was that I hope they're all right."

"You don't have to do this."

I let out a chuckle. "Do what?"

"Worry about other people. Care about what they're feeling." His jaw tenses. "It's clear that you've never suffered in life. You believe that there is kindness in everybody. You think a goodwill gesture can make everything right again."

I chuckle. "I don't see anything wrong with focusing on the positive and helping whoever I can."

"The world is an ugly place." He glares at me. "You were witness to that the night you were mugged."

I stand in place, toe-to-toe with him, never breaking our gaze.

"This date you're about to go on will disappoint you, Juliet."

I shake my head. "Don't talk about my date."

"You're expecting him to sweep you off your feet." His hand hovers just over the center of my chest. "Do you think he'll be the one who will steal your heart, protect it, honor it?"

I don't give him the satisfaction of a response.

"Do yourself a favor and skip it."

"Why would I do that?"

"It's a waste of your time."

"It's not," I argue, out of principle, not out of a desire to defend Slate.

"When was the last time a man satisfied you, Juliet?" His eyes flare wide.

Confused, I push. "What do you mean? Are you asking me when was the last time a man satisfied me emotionally or in bed?"

He laughs. It's curt and edged with a cruel note. "Emotionally, Juliet? Let's be brutally honest here. That's not what you're looking for, is it? You want to be satisfied in bed. You want a man who understands every nuance of your movements. You crave a man who hears the echoes of your desires in your moans and your screams. You want a man who knows how to fuck."

Stunned, I stare into his eyes. "Kavan."

"Juliet." My name slides off his lips, wrapped in a groan. "Slate won't fuck you like that. You know that he won't."

My hand itches to slap him, but I hold back. "I'm going on my date."

I turn to leave, determined to walk out of this penthouse with my head held high.

I don't know how we ran so far off course so fast, but I do

know that hearing Kavan Bane talking about fucking has set my body on fire.

I have to shake this off.

I need to come back here tomorrow focused on my objective. I'll gather the research I need to write an article so I can go back to the life I had before I met Mr. Bane.

CHAPTER TWENTY-SEVEN

KAVAN

"SURPRISE!"

It's just as it sounds. Three male voices all yelling one annoying-as-fuck word at me as soon as I walk into the private dining room at Sérénité.

I was lured here under false pretenses.

I glare at the man responsible for that.

Harrison Keene pitches a wink in my direction.

A goddamn wink of his eye while Graham and Sean laugh.

"What the fuck?" I mutter. "Are we twelve?"

"Twenty-nine and feeling fine," Sean corrects me in the most Sean way possible with a drink in his hand and a party hat of some sort on his head.

Am I dreaming this shit right now?

"I'm leaving," I announce.

"That's not happening, Bane." Graham approaches with a

bottle of beer in his hand. "The surprise isn't really for you, is it?"

That's a riddle I can't solve, so I get straight to the point. "What the hell is going on?"

Graham steps closer. "Tonight is the night we break the news."

"What news?" Harry asks from where he's standing. "I thought you said I was supposed to call Bane and tell him it was urgent so we could surprise him."

That's exactly what he did, and in my twisted tragedy-expecting mind, I thought it involved Harry's health since he's been in the hospital a few times in recent years.

"Is this just one of our monthly Buck Boys dinners?" Sean questions Graham as he tears the paper hat from his head.

I'd be happy if I never heard us referred to in that way again. We may have attended The Buchanan School, but we don't need to carry the undesirable moniker of being *Buck Boys* forever.

It's a tradition started before our time that should have died the day after it was born.

"Can't you just call them dinners?" I direct that at Sean.

He shoves a drink in my hand. "You look like you could use this."

"You have no idea," I say before I empty half the glass in one swallow.

"Why did I have to lure Bane here?" Harry gets to the subject at hand by getting in Graham's face. "You told me it was a surprise celebration, Locke."

Graham is still sporting the same broad smile he had when he told me Trina is expecting.

Suddenly, this all makes sense.

I check each of my friends' hands to make sure everyone has a drink.

I'll do the honors because if Graham wanted to, it would have happened by now.

He's wrought with emotion. I see it in his face.

I lift my glass in the air. "We are here for Graham, gentlemen. Our dearest and most annoying friend is going to be someone's father. Here's to the kid that has to put up with that."

Sean and Harrison exchange a look before they turn to Graham.

"It's true," he says in a relatively calm voice. "You're looking at a future girl dad."

Glasses clink, my friends hug each other, and I take it all in.

I wouldn't have missed this for the world, yet, part of me wishes I had just a moment more with Juliet earlier.

I pushed her in a way that I had no right to, but she pushed back, and that only served to spark something inside of me.

I want her.

I want to pin her to the wall and fuck her until my name falls from her lips.

"Thanks for handling that," Graham breaks into my thoughts with a pat on my back. "One day, all of us will be watching our kids play together."

He knows that's not in the cards for me, but I give him this moment.

"I'm hungry." Harry yanks on the back of a chair next to a table set up for the four of us. "Let's eat."

I take a seat with my friends, wondering what Juliet is doing with her new friend.

Slate.

"THERE SHE IS, SIR." Drew points a finger at the windshield of the SUV we're currently sitting in.

I left Sérénité with every intention of going home, but when Drew pulled up to the curb, and I got into the car, the lingering scent of Juliet's perfume hit me.

Drew drove her home earlier, while Alcott handled driving me to the restaurant in the BMW that spends most of its time in the basement garage in my building.

I take it out occasionally when I want to escape the city for a weekend.

I drive to wherever the road takes me. Often it's one of the smaller towns in upstate New York where no one has time to bother with reading books about sons murdering their billionaire fathers.

I'll spend a weekend hidden away in a Bed and Breakfast that accepts cash as payment.

"That must be Slate," he deduces based on the fact that the guy is walking next to Juliet.

I asked him to drive me here so we could park across the street from Juliet's apartment.

It's not logical, but neither is what I've been feeling brewing inside of me since I cornered her at my penthouse and asked what she's expecting from this date.

For some goddamn reason, I feel a pressing need to see what this Slate person looks like.

I grip the backrest of the front passenger seat to pull myself forward so I can peer out of the windshield.

Drew leans back as if he's trying to duck out of view. I'm not sure why given that we are parked near the end of the street.

There are thousands of vehicles in Manhattan that look

identical to this one. Hell, there are probably two parked within twenty-five feet of us.

She's not going to spot us.

I watch as Juliet, dressed in jeans, a cardigan, and flats, walks next to a man wearing glasses.

They are on the approach to her building.

"She mentioned him when I drove her home," Drew announces. "It seemed like she was pretty excited about this."

"Stop talking."

He nods. "I'm just saying that she seems like a great girl, and she deserves to find someone who can make her happy."

"Shut up, Drew."

Finally, he quiets enough that I swear to fuck I can hear every single thump of my heart inside my chest.

"You do not mention this to her. Understood?"

He nods.

I keep my gaze pinned to Juliet as they stop in front of her building. I should tell Drew to start the car to take me home, but I don't.

I stare at Juliet as she looks up and into the face of a guy who just took her on a date. He leans down. I curse inwardly, and then she turns her face a touch so his lips graze her cheek.

Slate has been denied a good night kiss.

"Ouch," Drew whispers.

I don't say anything as Juliet says something to Slate before he turns and walks away.

That sets me back on the seat with an unexpected charge of relief settling over me. I yank my phone out of my pocket to check the source of the buzzing that has been non-stop for the past five minutes. It's a string of texts from Graham thanking me for showing up tonight.

"Oh, shit," Drew says. "Sir, look."

I glance up to see Juliet headed straight for us.

She crosses the street in a sprint, and as soon as she's on the sidewalk next to the SUV, she raps her knuckles on the back passenger door window.

I lower it down, both annoyed and amused that I've been caught red-handed.

As soon as my face is in clear view, Juliet points a finger at me. "Your surveillance skills are shit."

I let out a laugh.

She sets both hands on her hips. "Oh my god, are you laughing? You know how to laugh?"

Drew chuckles but doesn't say a word.

"How was the date, Juliet?" I ask with a smirk.

"How's Harry?" she counters. "My bleeding heart wants to know."

I catch her eye with mine. "Harry is just fine."

"Good." She glances at her building. "I'm going home. I'll see you in the morning, Mr. Bane."

Before I have a chance to respond, she bends her knees to see into the car. "Goodnight, Drew."

"Night, Juliet."

I get nothing more as she takes off toward her apartment without looking back.

CHAPTER TWENTY-EIGHT

JULIET

"HOW WAS YOUR DATE, JULIET?"

I'll answer the question this time since it's my sister asking. I drop my purse on the couch before I shrug out of the cashmere cardigan Margot let me borrow.

I wanted to keep my outfit simple yet sophisticated, so the cardigan was the perfect touch.

"He's not for me," I sum up.

Margot glances to where I'm standing.

I can tell that she got home just a few minutes before me. She's in the kitchen with her hip propped against the counter as she eats leftover quiche.

"No spark?" she asks.

"Nope," I respond, wondering if there might have been a spark at another time.

All I could think of throughout dinner with Slate was the heated conversation I had with Kavan before I left the penthouse.

I kept replaying his words over and over again in my mind.

"*You crave a man who hears the echoes of your desires in your moans, and your screams. You want a man who knows how to fuck.*"

All of it is true.

I want that and more.

My dinner with Slate was fun. He talked sports and I listened. I can tell that we'd make great friends, but anything beyond that won't happen for us.

"How's work?" Margot asks as she takes another bite of food. "We haven't talked about that recently? Are you working on a new assignment?"

I nod. "I am. It's top secret."

Swallowing, she chuckles. "Aren't they all?"

"They are," I affirm with a quick nod of my chin. "How is work for you?"

"Brutal," she confesses before she picks up a glass of wine to take a sip. "I love it though. I wouldn't trade it for the world."

I wouldn't trade a moment like this for the world.

She's relaxed. She didn't text me twelve times during my date to see if I was okay. She limited that to twice.

"Do you want to watch the Duke do some naughty stuff?" She wiggles her brows.

"I'd love to." I gesture to the hallway. "I'm going to throw on some sweatpants, and make a bowl of popcorn."

"I'm all for that." She glances down at the designer dress she's wearing. "I'm sorry he wasn't the guy for you, Juliet."

"Don't be," I smile as I approach her. "Isn't part of the fun of finding the one, dating other guys?"

"If you say so." She laughs.

"I like it here," I whisper. "New York has been good to us so far, hasn't it?"

Her eyes mist over. "Other than that time you rescued a woman from a mugger, you mean?"

Her defenses are starting to melt, so I can't confess that I was that woman. I may need to take that to my grave.

"I'm proud of you, Juliet." A tear trails down her cheek. "You're so brave, and fearless."

I reach up to swipe the tear away. "So are you."

"New York really is starting to feel like home to me too," she admits. "I may never master the subway but that's what rideshares are for, right?"

"Right."

"Get changed so we can forget about everything but the Duke."

Nodding, I head to my bedroom.

I can't forget about everything.

Kavan came here to watch me with Slate. Either he doubts I can take care of myself, or jealousy speared him tonight.

My heart wants to believe it's the former, even though my common sense is telling me it's the latter.

"GOOD MORNING, JULIET," Nigel says cheerfully as I enter the penthouse with Alcott by my side.

"Hey, Nigel!" I raise a hand in greeting. "You're looking sharp today."

He's dressed as he usually is in a suit with a white button-down shirt and a patterned tie.

"As are you," he reciprocates the compliment.

My look isn't sharp. It's as dull as a marshmallow and just as comfortable.

I'm in jeans, a pink sweater, and a black blazer.

I overslept, so I had to hop in the shower quickly, put on a spot of make-up and get dressed in the span of twenty minutes.

Drew was waiting for me on the sidewalk in front of the building with a coffee. I thanked him profusely before I crawled into the waiting SUV and devoured every berry in sight.

I'm hoping that the linen napkin I used before I exited the SUV caught every spot of red and pink that was lingering on my lips.

"Is he already working?" I question Nigel. "I was hoping to get in a solid few hours of interview time today."

"He's running late."

Huh? How does one run late when they sleep in the same penthouse they work in? Is Kavan's bedroom so far from his office that he waits for Alcott to piggyback him there?

I hold in a laugh at the imagined image of that.

"You look amused," Nigel says. "What's on your mind, Juliet?"

I glance to where Nara is approaching with a coffee in her hand.

These people definitely know how to accommodate my coffee addiction.

I take the mug and thank her for the trouble.

She smiles. "I'm preparing the lunch menu, Juliet. Any special requests you'd like included within the options?"

Nigel's brows perks up but he doesn't say anything.

I lean closer to her and lower my voice. "Peanut butter and jelly sandwiches, please."

She looks at me with an expression that I can only classify as horror mixed with confusion. "What?"

"I'll take responsibility for it," I assure her. "You like PB and J sandwiches, Nigel, don't you?"

"Love them." He smiles.

Nara laughs before she starts back toward the kitchen.

"I'm going to head to my office to twiddle my thumbs," I announce. "When Mr. Bane is ready, can you tell him that I'm eager to get started?"

Nigel's gaze drifts over my shoulder. "You can tell him yourself."

I take the hint and glance back and *oh my fucking god.*

Wearing nothing but black sweatpants slung low over his hips, I catch sight of a very sweaty Kavan Bane standing barefoot less than ten feet behind me, holding a white towel in his hand.

His body is magnificent. Every muscled inch is utter perfection.

"Good morning, Juliet," he says in a way that is more a growl than a greeting.

I seriously wonder for a moment whether I might pass out from sensory overload.

"Good morning," I repeat unable to tear my gaze away from him.

He approaches me, and then brushes past me to head down a hallway. "I'll be ready for our interview shortly."

I stare at his back as he walks away.

"He was working out," Nigel states the obvious.

"I could tell," I mutter.

"You were about to go to your office, Juliet."

I nod. "Right. I'll go."

I turn and start walking.

"It's this way, dear," Nigel calls after me.

Shaking my head, I turn around and march down the corridor that leads to my office. "Thanks, Nigel."

"My pleasure, Juliet." He chuckles. "It's completely my pleasure."

CHAPTER TWENTY-NINE

JULIET

"WHAT HAVE you accomplished at Bane Enterprises that you're most proud of?" I read the question from the list I prepared on my phone.

"That's a question you'd ask someone at a job interview." Kavan crosses his arms. "Do better, Juliet."

My head pops up. I steal a glance at him but that lasts for less than two seconds before I pin my eyes to the screen of my phone again.

"Answer the question, Mr. Bane."

"No."

I've been avoiding looking at him since he walked into my office because all I can picture is his broad naked chest and the obvious bulge that was beneath his sweatpants.

I have to shake that image from my mind so I can get down to business. That would be the business of this interview that is going to vault my career to where I want it to be.

I suck in a deep breath and look at him. He's wearing a

black suit, shirt and tie. It might look morbid if he didn't have such beautiful blue eyes.

"That question helps me understand what motivates you," I explain.

"What motivates me is greed."

"Do you want me to put that in the article? Or should it be in the headline?"

"No one would be surprised by the notion that greed motivates me," he says with a straight face. "It motivates most people who are worth…"

"Billions of dollars." I roll my hand in the air. "You're not a cookie-cutter billionaire."

That lures a smile to his lips. "What is a cookie-cutter billionaire, Juliet?"

"You know the type." I lean back in my chair to cross my legs. "They're arrogant. They flash their wealth around. They have people waiting on them hand and foot. They bark out orders."

He taps a finger against the armrest of the chair as he listens.

"They've never cooked a meal for themselves. They've never flown commercial in their lives." I turn to look at him with a finger raised in the air. "Oh, wait. You are a cookie-cutter billionaire."

Amusement flits across his expression. "Is that how you view me?"

I think about that for a second. "No."

That's enough to pull another question out of him. "How do you view me, Juliet?"

"Honestly?"

He shifts in his chair. "Of course."

I look toward the open door of my office. "I view you as someone who is misunderstood. I think you're buried beneath something that borders on guilt but also edges pain. I believe that circumstances beyond your control formed this persona that you've had to carry with you for years."

His eyes hold tight to mine.

"The business is part of who you are, but it's not the whole of who you are." I keep going since he has yet to stop me. "I think that you're punishing yourself by sacrificing your chance at a fulfilling life because of someone else's lost life."

"My father?" he bites those two words out in a sharp tone. "Are you referring to him?"

Never breaking his gaze, I nod. "Yes."

He reaches forward to snatch my hand. He holds it tightly in his. "I warned you not to go there."

"Or what?"

"Drop it, Juliet."

I don't try and tug my hand free. I soften my stance, showing him that I'm not afraid. I refuse to be intimated by him.

"Creating a prison for yourself won't bring him back, Kavan."

"Stop!" His voice comes out curt with frustration lacing the tone.

"That's what you've done here." I swoop my free hand toward the doorway. "You live in a prison of your making. Don't you want to be free?"

Abruptly he stands and drops my hand. "Go home, Juliet."

I stand too. "No."

His eyes bore into mine. "You're sticking your nose where it doesn't belong."

Squaring my shoulders, I reach out to rest a hand on his

chest. “I promise that if you let it all out, there’s freedom on the other side of it.”

He wraps a hand around my wrist. “I told you to stop talking.”

“Make me,” I say in a childish way meant to taunt him.

“I will,” he growls before he tugs me closer, cups a hand around the back of my head, and seals his mouth over mine.

CHAPTER THIRTY

JULIET

MY HANDS JUMP up to grip the lapels of his jacket as he takes control of the kiss, tilting my head more.

He grinds against me with a groan spilling out from somewhere deep inside of him. I press closer, my lips, my body, all of me wanting to touch all of him.

His hand trails down my back to my ass. He holds me against him, against the outline of his swollen cock.

Suddenly, he breaks the kiss. His eyes wide with wonder, or maybe shock, he steps back. "Fuck, Juliet."

Yes, I want to. I want to fuck. Without thinking it through. With wild abandon.

Those words sit on my lips unsaid as he stares at me, through me, into the deepest recesses of my soul that no one has ever seen.

My lips quiver because there's an unspoken confession there I want him to hear.

I want this man to know my truth and I can't explain why I feel that.

Something inside of him speaks to me.

His eyes search my face.

With parted lips he lets out a heavy exhale. "I have a meeting."

The words hit as hard as a gut punch.

"Now?"

"Now," he repeats with conviction. "We'll continue this later…the interview later, but stay on topic."

How can he go from kissing me like that to slipping back into the buttoned up, uncaring businessman?

I felt need in that kiss, and a desire so strong that I thought he might tear my clothes off on the spot.

"Kavan," I whisper his name.

"I'll see you at lunch." Those words snap out of him with no emotion and not a single glance in my direction.

Then he's gone. With a brush of his bicep against my shoulder he's out of my office and stalking down the hall taking every one of his secrets and the tiniest sliver of my heart with him.

"WHAT THE HELL IS THIS?" Kavan opens the two pieces of white bread on the plate in front of him to look at the smeared peanut butter and strawberry jelly.

"My lunch choice," I say from across the table.

He picks up a piece of raw carrot. "You chose this too?"

I pick up one as well and snap off a bite. "Yep."

He looks toward Nigel who is enjoying his first bite of his sandwich with his eyes closed.

Kavan pushes his plate away. "I can't eat this."

Nigel pulls himself out of his sandwich fog to glance at his boss. "Try it, sir."

Kavan shakes his head. "This is ridiculous. I have a kitchen filled with the freshest ingredients money can buy and an award winning chef to prepare them, and you pick this?"

"It reminds me of my childhood," I confess.

Both men turn to look at me.

"My mom used to make these for my sister and I every Saturday." I run my fingertip over the crust of the bread. "On special occasions she'd cut out shapes in the bread."

"Like Christmas trees?" Nigel asks with gleaming eyes.

"Yes," I nod. "Hearts for Valentine's Day and turkeys right around Thanksgiving."

"That's endearing." Nigel glances at his half-eaten sandwich. "Do your parents live in New York, Juliet?"

"They're in London at the moment." I trail my gaze over the linen tablecloth. "Next month they'll move to Paris for a few months, then Rome."

"I see," he says while Kavan sits quietly.

"They're retired," I offer as an explanation although one isn't needed.

My parents raised my sister and I with love and grace. They didn't spoil us but made sure we had everything we needed. My mom taught us the basics of cooking. My father explained budgeting to us and, of course, he showed us how to defend ourselves.

That was important to him. *Very important.*

I take a bite of my sandwich.

"I would venture a guess that this is Nara's homemade strawberry jelly." Nigel runs a finger over his bottom lip. "It's running a close second to her lemon preserves."

"You should tell her," I encourage him. "Tell her how delicious this is."

Smiling, he pushes himself to his feet. "I'll do that right now. I'll be back in a moment."

I glance over to where Kavan is still seated with his hands resting on top of the table.

"You miss your parents, don't you, Juliet?" he asks.

"Very much," I admit.

I want to ask him if he misses his dad too, but I see it. I've seen it in his eyes since the moment we met.

Whatever happened in that hotel room in Miami shredded Kavan Bane's heart. I wish he'd let me help him put it back together again.

He drops his gaze to the plate in front of him. "I've never had a peanut butter and jelly sandwich."

I perk a brow. "Cookie-cutter billionaire."

Tilting his chin, he scoops up half of the sandwich in his hand before taking a huge bite. He chews, swallows, and then chases it with a sip from his water glass.

"What do you think?" I lean my elbows on the table. "It's good, right?"

His answer is a second bite and the hint of a smile.

CHAPTER THIRTY-ONE

KAVAN

JULIET WANTED that kiss as much as I did.

She told me that when she stepped closer, when her hands gripped the lapels of my jacket. It felt like a plea.

I thought about taking her to bed and fucking her mid-day with the sun streaming through my bedroom windows and onto her skin.

I stopped myself because I was falling.

Falling into something I hadn't planned. Falling into a desire so overwhelming that I was ready to speak my truth to a woman I barely know.

Yet, at the same time I feel as though I've known her forever.

I've never met anyone like her.

"Kavan." Her voice cuts through my thoughts. "Do you have a minute for me?"

I glance up to find her standing in the open doorway of my office.

It's late afternoon now.

I instructed Nigel to give her a copy of the latest board meeting with anything sensitive redacted.

If she's going to write an article about Bane Enterprises she needs, at the very least, minimal insight into the inner workings of the company.

"Of course, Juliet." I push to stand. "Come in."

She does just that, closing the door behind her.

That's a dangerous move considering I want nothing more than to kiss her again.

Hell, I do want more.

I want to strip her, bend her over my desk and slide my cock inside what I can only imagine is her very sweet, tight pussy.

"It's about this." She waves a piece of paper in her hand. "Not to be rude, but some of the board members are assholes."

I don't need proof of that on a piece of paper. I live it.

"I won't argue that point, but keep it out of the article."

She plops her round ass in one of the chairs that face my desk. "I've researched the holdings of Bane Enterprises for the past three years. I can see where there might be some concern, but you have acquired several businesses that are showing steady growth."

I sit back down in my chair. "I'm aware."

"Why aren't any of the financial magazines reporting on that?" She sets the paper on my desk. "You bought that video game company and now it's making serious bank."

"Serious bank?" I ask, suppressing the amusement I feel.

"Loads of cash," she says with a roll of her eyes. "There's also that print-on-demand greeting card company."

"It's making serious bank too," I say with a straight face.

She nods. "Those are incredible success stories. You took

those businesses and brought them back from the brink. Both of them are now multi-million dollar profit machines for Bane Enterprises."

"That's one way of putting it."

"You kept the owners on board," she points out. "Why has no one interviewed them about how you've changed their lives?"

I fold my hands together on top of my desk. "Because both of the former owners are your age, Juliet. They don't give a shit about anything but their bottom line. They're immune to everything else. No reporter wants that as a headline."

Her brow furrows. "What do you mean? Everyone wants to hear about success at that level."

I shake my head. "I assure they don't when the alternative is…"

Her gaze lands on my face as my voice trails.

She takes a deep breath. "When the alternative is all the failures related to what happened in the past."

"Exactly." I glance toward a window.

"This office is nothing like your real office."

I turn back to face her. "What?"

"This office is so much nicer than your office in the Bane Enterprises building." Her fingers run a path over the edge of my glass desk. "This is modern, and warm. You even have a picture of you and three men in here."

I don't need to ask what picture she's talking about.

"Is Harry there?" Her finger wags in the air toward a framed photograph of Sean, Graham, Harrison and I on a shelf behind my desk.

"Second from the left."

She squints. "Is he a cookie-cutter billionaire too?"

"He does all right. Why?"

"You can tell a lot about an interview subject by the company they keep." She glances at the picture again. "Are they your friends, Kavan?"

"Yes."

A smile greets me when she finally looks into my eyes again. "Good. Everyone needs friends they can count on."

My desk phone rings breaking the moment.

She glances at it. "I suppose I have to leave to preserve that Bane mystique thing you have going on?"

I ignore the call. "That Bane mystique thing? Is that tied to my status as a cookie-cutter billionaire?"

"Might be." She bounces to her feet. "I'll go see Nara and check what's on the dinner menu."

"Let her make the suggestions, Juliet."

"Or I might request chicken nuggets and curly fries, Bane."

I watch her leave my office, transfixed not only by the gentle sway of her ass as she walks but by her determination to never back down.

She's a force to be reckoned with and she's heaven to kiss.

That's a combination that could take the strongest of men to their knees.

CHAPTER THIRTY-TWO

KAVAN

I EXIT my office near six expecting to see Juliet in the main living area with Nigel, but that's not what I find.

Nigel is alone looking through what looks like pictures of birds on his phone.

I suppose there's some truth to the fact that there are clues everywhere about the people in our lives.

"Sir!" He bounces to his feet as soon as he spots me. "How did your final call of the day go?"

"Fine," I lie.

I spoke to the owner of a global sporting gear company that I've been trying to acquire for the past few months. He was adamant that he couldn't sell to Bane Enterprises after reading that fucking *The Bad Bane* book. He had the audacity to quote passages from it that he thinks are relevant to how I run the business.

I assured him the book was laced with lies and bullshit.

He told me to go to hell and hung up on me.

It's just another random afternoon in my world.

"Where's Juliet?" I start toward her office. "Is she still working?"

"She left an hour ago, Mr. Bane."

I turn to look at Nigel. "What?"

"She got a call and explained that she had to meet someone for dinner." He sighs. "I don't know the details, sir. She did say that she chose our dinner from Nara's suggested menus."

"All right," I say as disappointment tears through me.

I thought Slate was a no-go, but maybe a quick peck on the cheek is akin to first base for Juliet.

If it is, we rounded third base on the kiss we shared this morning in her office.

"She did want me to tell you that she won't be by tomorrow."

More fucking bad news.

"Why?"

"She has an appointment to tend to." He glances back at the screen of his phone. "She wasn't forthcoming with details. I didn't push."

He should have pushed.

Having her here, inside these four walls, has been welcome. It didn't begin that way, but I enjoy having her in my home.

"It works out well, though." Nigel says with a cheery note in his tone.

I snap my head to look in his direction. "How so?"

"The board called an emergency meeting for tomorrow afternoon I just received a secret memo about it."

As if on cue, my phone buzzes in my pocket.

I yank it out to see the notification of the meeting.

For fuck's sake.

"Fine," I growl the word out. "Tell Nara I want dinner in my office. You're free to go home, Nigel."

"I'm going to do just that." He turns toward the foyer. "I'll miss her too, sir."

I face him again. "Who?"

"Juliet," he says with a grin. "She's brought something to this place that has been sorely missing."

I ignore that because I can't acknowledge it out loud.

"Once her article is complete, we may never see her again."

"She's not moving across the globe, Nigel," I point out, frustrated with this conversation. "She works a block from here."

"That's close for me," he agrees with a nod of his head. "It's a world away for you though, isn't it?"

Without a word to him, I head down the corridor before I slam my office door behind me.

FIVE FUCKING HOURS.

I spent five fucking hours listening to the board drone on about everything that isn't going right.

Nigel took it upon himself to point out where the company is making profits, but the goddamn board was stuck on the deal with the sporting goods company that collapsed yesterday.

It's yet another mark against me.

I sat through that hell until I called it adjourned.

The chairman of the board attempted to pull rank to keep me in my seat, but fortunately, the other board members were in a rush to head home to home-cooked meals and I suspect rendezvous with mistresses, so we called it a day.

Now, I'm on the sidewalk in front of the Bane tower about to head home through the alley that has become a shortcut of sorts for me.

I turn up the collar on suit jacket to help with the biting wind that has swept over the city since this afternoon.

A couple strolling by do a double take when they see my face, but they move on whispering something to each other.

I glance to my left to a line of people waiting to gain access to a restaurant.

At one time in my life, I would have leapfrogged that line while holding tightly to my mother's hand.

It's her favorite in the city, and that's not because they serve a steak that melts in your mouth like butter.

It's one of those places that paparazzi used to converge on to snap pictures of New York's wealthiest as they were on their way to eat an overpriced meal and consume a bottle of wine that costs more than most people in this city pay in rent for a month.

I step closer to the curb to get a better look at those in line because I recognize someone.

Her hair is as red as I remember. Her profile showcases the same small bump on her nose that she's always hated, yet never took that extra step to fix.

I turn away briefly because it's been years since my mother has spoken to me, but something draws my gaze back to her.

That's when I see the woman she's with.

She's wearing a black lace dress that accentuates every curve of her frame. On her feet are nude heels. She turns slightly, sending her brown hair whipping against the side of her beautiful face.

It's Juliet.

"Fuck," I mutter as two women walk past me.

"I'm game," one calls out to me. "You did say you want to fuck, right?"

Her blonde-haired friend giggles. "I'm in. He looks like he can handle both of us."

I can, and I have taken two women to bed at once.

I wave them away as I head down the sidewalk, my blood boiling, my heart thumping against my ribcage.

"Juliet!" Her name snaps off my tongue laced in anger, confusion, and an ounce of disbelief.

Her head turns slowly. "Kavan?"

"Kavan," my mother repeats my name but the warmth that was once there is long gone. "What are you doing here?"

I don't acknowledge her. I head straight for Juliet.

"Kavan," she says my name again, but nothing follows that.

I reach for her. Grabbing hold of her hand I tug her toward me. "You're coming with me."

She doesn't fight me. Not a word leaves her pink hued lips.

She looks up at me with those hazel eyes that are rimmed in dark shadow, liner, and a thick coat of mascara.

"Where?" she whispers.

I don't answer. I can't. I tug on her hand and lead her into the alley, not once looking back.

CHAPTER THIRTY-THREE

KAVAN

"LEAVE!" My voice booms through the penthouse. "Everyone out."

Nara hurries out of the kitchen and rushes toward the door without a glance in our direction.

Alcott rounds a corner and does the same.

I stand in place, watching them until the door closes behind them.

That's when I finally release Juliet's hand.

I can't look at her.

She was standing on the sidewalk, wide-eyed and broad-smiled while talking to my mother.

I stalk across the room to the bar cart. With steady hands I pour myself two fingers of Macallan 15. I down it in one gulp. Then I pour another splash of it into the tumbler and take that in a single swallow.

"Kavan," Juliet whispers.

"Quiet," I growl.

"It's not what you think," she says, her voice louder.

That can only mean one thing. She's on the approach from behind me.

I stare out at the lights of the city through one of the windows. "Not now, Juliet."

"Now," she insists. "I reached out to her because…"

I turn on my heel. "Because you wanted her to fill your head with her version of events?"

She sets her purse on the couch. "No. I'm writing an article on Bane Enterprises. She's a major stockholder. I was simply gaining her perspective on where the business stands today."

"You reached out to her," I point an accusatory finger at her, willing her to stay in place.

She stops mid-step. "I had to."

A bitter laugh laced with the pain of the past five years escapes me. "Bullshit."

Her gaze travels over my face. "It's my job, Kavan."

"Your job?" I repeat. "Your job is to go behind my back to speak to someone who has done nothing but drag me through the press for something…"

I stop myself, because *goddammit*, some people will swear that the truth will set you free, but it won't do that for me.

It will release me from one type of prison straight into another.

Shame is something a man can learn to live with.

Guilt is far worse a sentence in my opinion.

"Something…" Naturally she pushes for more.

"You should have run it by me first, Juliet."

"I was doing my job," she insists with a stamp of her heel on the floor.

I turn back to the bar cart and pour another finger of

whiskey. I swallow it, letting it burn a slow path down my throat.

"Look at me, Kavan."

I look up at the window to find her there. It's her reflection, but in this moment, with my sins so close to the surface, it's all I can handle.

"Do you want to know what I think?"

"No," I answer curtly. "I want to know what you were thinking when you called her and asked her to meet you."

"I think you're in a pain so debilitating that you can't find a path out of it."

"You're not a shrink, Juliet."

"I'm a journalist," she says with pride lacing the words. "My job is to get to the heart of the story and report it. I was doing that tonight."

I turn to face her. "The heart of the story? You're writing a fluff piece on my company, Juliet. You're not going to win a Pulitzer for it."

Her left eyebrow inches up just a touch. "You're an asshole. I'm leaving."

Panic races through me as she reaches to pick up her purse. "Juliet."

The only sound echoing through the penthouse is the click of her heels as she heads toward the door.

I sprint around her to block her path.

"Move." She pushes a hand on my chest. "Get the hell out of my way."

I hold her hand on my chest, over my heart. "Stop."

"Stop what?" she snaps. "Stop doing my job? Stop trying to help you? Stop caring about you?"

That's all it takes for the dam within me to burst.

I yank her closer, pull on the back of her hair to line her mouth up with mine and I crash my lips into hers.

WE STUMBLE to my bedroom with me tugging on her waist while she holds tightly to my face, kissing me with wild abandon.

I'm a man hungry for something I've never tasted before.

I've never kissed a woman with this much desire fueling it.

All of the control I possess has slipped away under her touch. I can't think. I can only feel and my need for her is trumping everything else.

I push her backward.

She falls onto my bed. Her gaze travels over my face, and beyond to the darkened shadows of the place I retreat to at the end of the day.

"Kavan," she whispers my name.

I'm on my knees because I can't control what I'm feeling. I haul her dress up to her waist to reveal a pair of black silk panties.

"You're soaking wet," I grit those words out as I settle between her legs. "So fucking wet for me."

She lets out a sound that fills the silence in the room.

I dive down, my tongue trailing over the silk for my first taste, but it's torturous. There's a hint of her sweetness, but it's not enough.

I curve a finger on each side of her panties and pull them down.

I tug harder, sliding them over her toned legs until she's bare.

"I...Kavan…please."

She doesn't need to plea.

I do. I need to plea for mercy. Plea for the honor of pleasing this woman.

I push her thighs apart with my hands to reveal her core.

With the soft glow trailing in from the lights of the city, she's a vision. "You're so beautiful, Juliet. This is so beautiful."

Her hands flail for something to grip onto so I guide one to my lips. I kiss her palm softly. "I want this."

"I want this," she repeats on stuttered breaths.

I slide my tongue over her cleft, finally tasting her.

I eat her with abandon. Soft licks and the nip of my teeth on her clit draw her closer to the edge.

I slide a finger into her, then another, marveling at how snug she is.

With my cock aching in my pants, I take her swollen pink nub between my lips and suck.

Her hands thread through my hair as she moans again and again.

It's a symphony of her pleasure, and as she soars into an orgasm, she cries out. I stay in place kissing her inner thighs while I whisper into her skin that she's just given me the greatest gift of my life.

CHAPTER THIRTY-FOUR

JULIET

I STARE at him while he strips down to absolutely nothing.

His body is truly magnificent.

I've been nude since he tugged my dress over my head after he ate me to an orgasm.

He wanted seconds, but I pulled at his shirt to get him up and over me.

Then I kissed him softly, tasting myself on his mouth.

"Your body is incredible," I whisper.

He glances at me from where he's standing near his bed. "I'll take the compliment, Juliet, but if we're going to discuss beautiful bodies, you are divine."

I roll onto my back. "Get a condom."

"My bossy little lover." He laughs. "She wants to be fucked."

"Hard," I draw the word out slowly.

His hand strokes the length of his cock. "What if I want to eat you again?"

I'd want nothing more if I had already felt him inside of me, but there's an ache that his mouth and lips can't chase away.

"I've wanted to fuck you for a long time," I confess.

He turns to face me head on, with his hand still running slow strokes over his erection. He's large. His balls are heavy.

The man is powerful in every single way.

"I've wanted to fuck you for longer." He takes a step closer to the bed. "I wanted you when you walked into my office that first day."

"You didn't."

He huffs out a laugh. "I did. I wanted you then. I want you more now."

I part my legs. "So come get me."

He moves toward a cabinet across the room. I admire his ass as he does.

"You're just as impressive from the back."

There's a slight shake of his head. "As are you."

I roll onto my stomach. "You like me like this, do you?"

When he turns back around he's sheathing his cock. "No. Not like that, Juliet."

"How then?"

He crawls onto the bed, flipping me over with ease. "Like this. I want to look at you when I fuck you."

My breath catches when he shoves my legs apart. His eyes trail over my body.

"Stop looking," I whisper. "Start fucking."

He moves between my legs, guiding his cock to my core.

He teases me, stroking the tip over my clit. "You want this, Juliet."

"Yes," I say, staring into his brilliant blue eyes. "I want you."

With a sudden thrust forward, he's inside of me. It's too much, so much, that I cry out.

"Easy," he says, leaning forward to pepper my forehead with kisses. "Deep breaths."

He moves gently, his eyes never leaving mine.

I rock my hips slowly, adjusting to his size. "It feels so good."

He drops his head to my neck. "You're so good. So fucking good."

He fucks me like that with soft whispered words, holding onto every ounce of self-control that he has.

"Let go," I whisper. "Let go, Kavan. Take me."

He does. He ups the pace. Hard thrusts of his hips while his hands roam my body. Strong fingers twisting my nipples and digging into my thighs until I cry out.

He does too with a groan ripped from the deepest part of him. He fills the condom with shaking thrusts before he falls onto me to rest his lips against my neck.

"Juliet." My name escapes him. "My beautiful Juliet."

I close my eyes to fight off the flood of emotions that hit me like a battering ram.

I want nothing more than to be his Juliet, and at least for tonight, I am.

"PEANUT BUTTER AND JELLY SANDWICHES." Kavan lets out a low chuckle. "Very funny, Juliet."

I bounce up to my tiptoes to kiss his mouth. "I think you pronounced that wrong. The term is very delicious, Juliet."

He catches my chin in his hand before he kisses me again, but this one is slow and lingering. I can taste the sweetness of his breath and smell our sex on his skin.

He fucked me once, stripped off the condom, ate me, and fucked me again.

It took hours, but felt like it wasn't long enough.

I want more. I want more of all of it.

"You're delicious," he says as he stares at my lips.

I fall back to my bare feet as I stare up at him. "Thank you for letting me borrow your shirt, Bane."

He glances down at the black button-down shirt I slipped on after I crawled out of his bed. It's much too large for me, but I only buttoned two buttons mid-stomach and I rolled up the sleeves far enough that my hands are visible.

"I should thank you for that," he counters. "Do you know how breathtaking you are, Juliet?"

I know I'm beautiful. I've been told that my entire life and there was a time when I thought that defined me.

It doesn't, but I like knowing Kavan sees my outer beauty as well as what's inside of me.

I look into his eyes. "One day I'll win a Pulitzer Prize."

His eyes hold mine. "You will. I'm sorry for that remark. It was out of line."

Not wanting to weigh this moment down with what happened earlier, I smile. "Eat your sandwich, Kavan."

"What happens if I don't?"

I skim a hand over his chest, down his stomach until it stops just above his boxer briefs. "I won't suck you off tonight."

He lunges forward toward the dining room table and the meager meal I prepared for us. "Give me that sandwich. I'll eat ten if it means I get to feel your pillow soft lips wrapped around me."

CHAPTER THIRTY-FIVE

KAVAN

EXHAUSTED AND SATIATED, I tug on Juliet's hair. "I'm good. I'm so good."

Her eyes bolt up to meet mine. "You're not kidding."

I watch as she swipes the back of her hand over her mouth. "That was nice."

Nice?

I huff out a laugh. "Nice is a picnic in the park. That blowjob was fucking incredible."

That lures her into my lap on the couch.

She crawls up and onto me, settling over my cock. "What would you know about picnics in parks?"

I adjust her in my lap because being this close to her is too much. I'm already hardening even though I blew a load down her throat less than two minutes ago.

"I know it's a thing people do."

"Such a cookie-cutter billionaire." She swats my shoulder. "People? I happen to love picnics in the park, Kavan."

"You do?"

I needed to know that. I don't know why but that feels important. Suddenly, many things do.

"What's your favorite color, Juliet?"

She leans back to study my face. "Why?"

"Answer the question."

"Purple." Her fingertips tap against my shoulder. "Yours?"

I stare at her.

"You have one, right?" she questions. "Kavan, you must have one."

"Hazel. It's hazel."

The corners of her eyes crinkle as she smiles. "Are you saying that because my eyes are hazel? Are you hoping to get lucky again tonight?"

"I will get lucky again tonight," I say as I snake a hand under the hem of the shirt. "You're not leaving here until I fuck you again."

She cups a hand over my cheek. "You don't smile enough."

I move my hand up her thigh, settling it so my fingertips brush against her pussy. "Smiling is overrated."

"It's not," she argues. "If you could see yourself when you smile, you'd do it all the time."

She's wrong. I don't want to see myself smile.

When I do I'm reminded of the last picture ever taken of my father and I. Nigel snapped it on a beach in Miami hours before my father drew his last breath.

I close my eyes. "Juliet."

I sense her lips hovering over mine. "It's okay to be happy again."

I reach forward until my lips touch hers for a soft kiss. "I'm not sure that's true."

She taps my chin. "Look at me, Kavan."

I slowly open my eyes to see the gold flecks in her irises. The color of her eyes is as unique as she is.

"Are you happy tonight?" she asks.

"I'm satisfied."

"You're not." She shakes her head. "I sense you're the type of man who is never satisfied."

That may have been true before she walked into my life.

I feel a sense of satisfaction I haven't before. I'm content.

"Are you happy?" she asks again.

"I'm happy I met you," I say as a compromise.

"Even though I make you eat PB and J, and I push you beyond your comfort zone?"

I inch my fingers up to skim them over her pussy. "Even then, Juliet."

Her eyes close on a heavy breath. "You're going to make me come again, aren't you?"

I press my lips to the soft flesh of her neck as I slide a finger into her channel. "Again and again."

THIS NIGHT HAS BEEN one I'll never forget, but as Juliet slips back into her dress, I take a deep breath.

What brought us here hasn't been resolved and I don't want to leave it until morning.

"Juliet." I shove my hands into the front pocket of my jeans as I watch her try to slip on one shoe. "I want to talk about something."

She holds up a hand. "Help me for a second."

I do that without hesitation, but instead of giving her a hand to balance on, I drop to one knee.

I gaze up at her as I slide her shoes onto her feet.

We stay like that for a moment until I pull myself upright again.

"I think I know what you want to talk about," she says softly. "Your mom."

I take a step back to not only gather my thoughts, but to breathe.

After tasting her skin, and being inside her, I'm struggling to think clearly.

That's not who I am after sex.

I fuck, I get dressed, I leave and I forget the encounter within days, often within hours.

These moments with Juliet will never leave me.

I already know that.

"Alvina Bane isn't who you think she is," I begin before I pause.

"I think she's a woman who abandoned her only child when he needed her the most," Juliet spits out.

That's my mother in a nutshell.

"I didn't meet with her because I wanted to hear her side about what happened to your family," she explains. "I met with her because she handed her voting proxy over to someone other than her son. I wanted to understand that and her motivations. I want to know how she thinks she fits into the future of the company because from where I'm standing right now, she doesn't."

I stare at her.

"That's my opinion, of course," she adds for good measure.

"I see."

"I don't think you know that she's spoken on record about you." She sighs. "I'm not going to quote any of it, but it made my blood boil. She has this brilliant, strong, beautiful son that she trashes at every turn."

I do know everything that my mother has said on and off record about me. I've never given it any weight because she was nowhere near Miami when my father died. She's never accepted my version of the events that happened that night, even when shown proof.

"I saw you two laughing outside the restaurant, Juliet."

That lures her closer to me again. Her hand lands on the center of my chest as she looks up and into my eyes. "If you disarm your enemy with laugher, they'll never see it coming."

I smile. "What exactly is it?"

"The attack," she explains with a grin. "In your mother's case, I wanted her to be comfortable so her truths would spill out."

"Her truths will never spill out."

Her fingers skim over the scruff covering my chin. "All of our secrets eventually come out."

"Do you have secrets, Juliet?"

She stares into my eyes and with a silent nod she confirms that she does.

"Tell me."

Her bottom lips trembles but she quiets it almost instantly with a bite of her teeth.

"Tell me," I repeat.

Her lips part, she sucks in a heavy breath and then drops her gaze. "That scarf you used to tie up the mugger was my favorite."

It's a diversion meant to lure a smile from me, but it's not the answer I was looking for.

"I have to get home." She spins around to face my bed. "Do I have everything?"

She has everything she came with, but she's leaving with more than that.

A piece of my heart is going with her.

I'm falling for this vibrant, sexy, stubborn, and fearless beauty.

I can't stop it. Hell, I don't want to, but I do want something.

I want her to confess her secrets to me, but I can't ask for that until I'm ready to confess mine to her.

CHAPTER THIRTY-SIX

JULIET

"HOW IS THAT ASSIGNMENT GOING?" Sinclair turns to look at me as we walk side-by-side down Broadway. "The one with the hot single arrogant guy."

I skirt around a couple that are so enamored with each other that they don't see us on the approach. "Good."

I rate it good even though the other night was the best sex of my life.

Since then, Kavan has been buried in work so we haven't had a chance to schedule more interview or personal time.

We have been texting and he did call to ask me not to speak to his mother until we've had a chance to discuss it more.

I agreed and before the call ended, he told me missed me.

I've been devoting myself to helping Margie at her office, as well as hanging out in my office at Marks Creative.

Mr. Marks popped his head in once to ask if I was making good progress.

I gave him a thumbs-up and a nod.

I'm making great progress on the article that focuses solely on the promising future of Bane Enterprises.

The article that Mr. Marks wants me to write that delves into Kavan's personal tragedy is still just a vision in my mind. I haven't been able to write one word because it feels like a betrayal to Kavan.

In a perfect world, Mr. Marks would grant me the honor of telling Kavan's story in a way that doesn't leave him in more pain than he already is.

"Good as in '*we haven't slept together yet*' or good as in '*he fucked me so hard that I was screaming*?'"

I bark out a laugh. "Sinclair!"

"Juliet," my name comes out of her with a trace of a giggle. "Inquiring minds need to know."

"Want to know," I correct her. "You know I can't give you any details on my current assignment."

"That's not a no." She gestures to a clothing store. "I've been eyeing up a dress in there. I'd like a second opinion on whether or not I should buy it."

Smiling, I link my arm around hers. "I'm in."

She pats my hand. "One day I'll find out who this mystery man is, right?"

I want her to.

I want what's happening between Kavan and me to last beyond the day I hand in my final article.

I think I might want it to last forever.

"MR. BANE WILL BE with you shortly, Juliet." Nigel eyes my outfit. "That dress is lovely. The color suits you."

I glance down at the fitted pink dress that I picked up the

day that Sinclair and I went shopping.

She opted for the exact same dress in blue. The color was a close match for her eyes.

When I tried it on in pink, she squealed. The smile on the face of the sales person told me that it was a solid investment.

We left the dress store and headed straight to a shoe store.

It was a day filled with shopping, girl talk, and then Italian food for dinner at a place called Calvetti's.

It was the perfect day for us to build on our blossoming friendship.

"It's new." I spin in a circle. "It's a bit bold for me, but I love it."

"As do I."

The rasp of that voice sends goose bumps scattering over my skin. It also turns me around in my heels.

Kavan is standing less than ten feet away from me.

"Hey, Bane."

He smiles. "Hey, Bardin. You do look lovely."

I rake him from head to toe. "You look different."

He skims a hand over the front of the grey sweater he's wearing. He's paired that with black slacks and wingtip shoes.

It's more casual than normal, but I like it.

"In a good way," he says.

I smile because it's not a question. The man knows he's hot-as-hell.

"Head to your office, Juliet." He gestures to the long corridor that leads to the offices, including mine. "I'll be in shortly."

I wait for him to move, but he doesn't, so I take the hint that he has something to discuss with Nigel.

Turning toward the corridor, I start walking to my office glancing back just once to catch Kavan's gaze pinned to me.

CHAPTER THIRTY-SEVEN

JULIET

I RUN my fingers over a card attached to a giftwrapped box on top of my desk.

My name is scrawled out in masculine handwriting.

I pick it up and study it.

That's all that's written on it but it already feels like a gift because I'm certain that Kavan wrote it by hand.

Unsure of whether I should open the beautifully wrapped gift without him, I take a seat behind my desk.

Something catches my eye near the doorway, so I turn to find Nara standing there with a cup of coffee in her hands.

"Good morning," I greet her.

"Hi, Miss Bardin." She places a linen napkin on my desk before she sets the coffee next to it. "Be careful. It's hot."

"Thank you and please call me Juliet."

"Juliet," she whispers. "You haven't opened the gift yet."

I glance at the pretty purple paper it's wrapped in and the

silver ribbon tied around it. "Do you know if it's from Mr. Bane? I think I should wait to open it until he's here."

"It is from Mr. Bane and he told me if I arrived to find it unopened, I should encourage you to open it."

That's all I need to hear.

As she exits my office, I bounce back to my feet, and untie the ribbon. With careful precision I open the giftwrap, wanting to preserve it.

It's a silly thing to do, but the card, wrapping paper, and ribbon are all a part of something Kavan chose just for me.

I take a deep breath before I open the square, flat box.

White tissue paper stands in the way of my gift and me, so I fold it back.

My breath catches in my throat when I see what's inside.

Before I can pick it up, I sense he's near. I glance at the doorway to find him there.

"Kavan." His name comes out wrapped in a tremor. "It's my scarf."

He stalks toward me to pull the black and white polka dot scarf from the box. "This one is a little different. It's silk and there is a special label sewn on it."

I snatch it from his hands. Turning it over and over I struggle to find the label.

When I do, I read the words stitched on it out loud. "If lost return to Juliet Bardin. Future Pulitzer Prize winner. Lover of PB and J."

My head falls back in laughter. "This is officially my favorite scarf now. Thank you. This is incredibly thoughtful of you."

He slides it from my hands to wrap it around my neck. "I know that your deepest secrets have nothing to do with scarves, Juliet."

I look into his eyes. "You're right."

His hands tug on the ends of the scarf to bring me closer so he can kiss me softly.

I melt into it, resting my hands on his chest. I feel the strong beat of his heart.

"Trust me to guard your secrets," he whispers.

Staring into his eyes, I reach up to cup his cheek in my hand. "Only if you trust me to guard yours."

His lips part, but no words escape him.

He kisses me again with so much tenderness that I lose my breath when it breaks.

"I love my gift," I confess softly, wanting to say more.

I want him to know how I feel.

I'm falling…hard, fast, and willingly in love with him.

"I'd give you the world if I could, Juliet."

I don't want that.

All I want is his heart and I don't know if that's something he'll ever give me.

I TYPE out the last word on my article detailing Kavan's vision for the future of Bane Enterprises.

It's not as thorough as I had wanted, but it's informative, and I know it will convey the message that Kavan wants it to.

People will see that under Kavan's guidance, Bane Enterprises has acquired several small companies that have become strong contenders within their relevant markets.

I accentuated that with quotes from the former owners of the video game and print-on-demand greeting card companies. When I interviewed them on the phone a few days ago, both had nothing but kind words about Kavan's commitment to following their visions when it came to the growth of the enterprises they had launched years before.

I stare at the screen of my laptop.

This is the article that I should hand in to Mr. Marks for his approval.

If I do that, it closes the door on the piece that I've been working on that is more personal and reaches beyond the scope of Kavan's business. I may never show that to anyone because it feels so intimate.

Sighing, I save the document and snap the cover of my laptop shut.

My favorite professor always told me to take a day to sit on your words before you show them to anyone, so that's what I'm going to do.

I hear footsteps on the approach down the corridor, so I glance toward the doorway.

Nigel pops his head in. "How are you doing, Juliet?"

"I think I'm going to call it a day."

He nods before he steals a glance over his shoulder. "If you could stay in your office for the next fifteen minutes, you'd have my eternal gratitude."

You can't say something like that to an investigative journalist and expect them to stay put.

"Why?" I ask with a sweet smile that I hope will lure the truth from Nigel.

"I can't say," he answers softly.

"You can say," I correct him. "You just don't want to."

He pops a finger in the air. "Touché."

"I could pretend I didn't hear you and wander out into the main living room," I suggest with a tilt of my chin. "It's not like I'm going to come across Mr. Bane doing something he shouldn't, right? Is he out there eating a frozen pizza or a candy bar?"

His hearty laughter fills the air. "Those are sights I'd long to see."

"Me too," I whisper.

He steps into my office far enough that he can close the door behind him. "May I speak frankly, Juliet?"

I cross my legs and turn toward him so he knows he has my full attention. "Please do."

He heads for the vacant chair and sits down. His fingers migrate to the pin on his lapel. Today it's a bluebird. The color of the rhinestones is vibrant against the dark material of his suit jacket.

"I've known Kavan for his entire life." His voice has a tremor in it. "I've watched him grow from a playful boy into a troubled teen, and now, into a man."

I nod.

"He has frozen his life in time." His gaze drops to his lap. "Before you came along, there was no joy in his eyes."

My eyes start to well with unshed tears. "He deserves to feel joy."

"He does." He nods curtly. "He truly does, Juliet."

I rest my hands on my desk. "I want to help him, Nigel."

"As do I." His eyes find mine. "I learned a very long time ago that pushing him will only cause him to retreat, but with you…with you, I see him opening up."

I smile. "You do?"

"He laughs with you." He lets out a chuckle. "Do you know how many years I waited to hear that again?"

"Too many."

He nods. "Yes. Too many."

"How do I help him open up to me?" I ask. "How can I make him see that he can trust me?"

Resting his forearms on his thighs, he scrubs one hand over his knee. "Dare I say love him, Juliet? I may be seeing something that isn't there, but I believe you're falling in love with Mr. Bane, and if you are, please love him with the understanding that beneath that gruff exterior, and hardened attitude, there is a broken man carrying a burden that is much too heavy for one person."

"I'm falling in love with him," I confess, for the first time. "I'll help him carry that burden."

He pushes off the chair to reach for my hand. "You are a gift, Juliet. Not only to Kavan, but to everyone who loves him."

I look into his face hoping that he sees the uncertainty I feel. "Nigel, do you think it's possible he's falling in love with me too?"

"He's fallen, Juliet." He pats the top of my hand. "He hasn't said a word to me, but it's those unspoken cues that tell me Mr. Bane is in love with you too."

CHAPTER THIRTY-EIGHT

Kavan

"I THOUGHT you were planning a surprise party for me, Mr. Bane."

I turn to find Juliet standing behind me with a sly smile on her face.

"A surprise party?" I question. "Does anyone actually like those things?"

She jerks a thumb toward the center of her chest. "This anyone does."

"Noted."

She approaches me with slow steps. "Nigel held me hostage in my office."

"He did, did he?"

"One he did is enough, or a did he." She laughs. "Sometimes you speak like a cookie-cutter…"

"Billionaire," I finish her sentence. "Do I fuck like one?"

That sends her gaze over my frame. "You're my first

billionaire. None of the other men I fucked were worth more than a hundred dollars."

I smile. "Good to know, but don't mention them again."

Her tongue trails a slow path over her bottom lip. "Because hearing about them makes you jealous?"

"Damn right," I admit.

"None of them had anything on you, Bane." Her eyes narrow. "You're hot, great in bed, and you're open to trying new things."

"I'm open to trying new things in bed?"

That lures a soft laugh from her. "Something tells me you've tried everything there is to try in the bedroom, and you may have even thought up a few new things."

"Why try new things when you're about to fuck the best thing that's ever happened to you?"

My words surprise me as much as they do Juliet.

Her hand jumps to the middle of her chest, so I add to the moment and point toward the dining room table. "I arranged something for you. It's a not a surprise party, but it's a little something."

She spins around to take a look and all I hear is a squeal before she sets off in that direction.

"Oh my god, Kavan. This is breathtaking."

It's beautiful, I suppose, but the only thing I've ever seen in my life that I consider breathtaking is her.

I scan the bouquets of purple flowers that were delivered a few minutes ago. All are exquisitely arranged in glass vases of varying heights.

"These are all for me?" She laughs as she turns to look at me. "There must be ten bouquets here."

"I didn't know what your favorite flowers are, so I chose the ones I thought you'd like."

"I love them." She moves to kiss me softly. "I love them so much. Thank you."

"I sent everyone home," I tell her.

She glances over her shoulder. "I thought Nara and Alcott lived here."

"I have an apartment one floor down that Nara lives in. Alcott lives a floor below that."

She shakes her head. "You own two other apartments in this building?"

I hold up a hand. "Wait. Are you going to tell me that's a cookie-cutter billionaire thing?"

"I'm going to tell you that it's a pretty sweet thing."

"I don't do sweet, Juliet." I chuckle. "Explain how it's sweet, though, because I don't see it."

"You do sweet, Bane. All the flowers are very sweet." She steps closer to me. "You don't see what's happening between Nara and Alcott?"

Lost in not only the conversation, but her eyes, I reach for her hand. "See what?"

"Nara and Alcott are in love, Kavan. I think you can sell one of those apartments."

I shake my head, convinced that I didn't hear that. "What?"

"They are in love," she says slowly.

I laugh. "Who the fuck told you that?"

Resting both of her hands on my shoulders, she looks into my eyes. "No one at first. I saw the way he looked at her. I watched how she'd stand close to him. Their hands would brush against each other."

Stunned, I hold back a smile. "You saw all of that?"

She nods. "There is this magic in the eyes of a man in love. When he looks at the woman who owns his heart, it's there. I saw it, and knew."

I want to ask her if she sees that same magic in my eyes when I'm looking at her. I feel it.

Jesus, do I feel it.

"I'll tell you a secret, Kavan."

"Tell me." The words leave me with hope that she'll bare herself to me.

I want to see into her soul.

She bounces up to her tiptoes to kiss me softly. "When he has saved up enough for a ring, Alcott is going to ask Nara to marry him."

I'd be pissed that the secret has nothing to do with her, but this is bringing her joy. She's radiant, happy, and excited for these two people that she only met recently. Granted she likely knows them better than I do, even though they've both been working for me for years.

"My bleeding heart is bursting with joy for them." She lets out a slight laugh. "Call me a romantic, but I think we should order something special for them for dinner tonight."

"You're a romantic," I call her. "I'll call Sérénité and have them deliver dinner for two to Nara's apartment. It's the nicer of the two."

"Maybe for four?" Her brows perk.

"We're not eating dinner with them, Juliet." I grab her waist with both hands. "I want you all to myself tonight."

"Order dinner for two for Nara and Alcott in their love pad." She smiles. "And another dinner for two in bed for us."

"Dinner in bed?" I ask, amused with the conversation, and frankly hard as fuck at the notion of doing anything in bed with her.

She spins around and fists her hair, pulling it up. "Unzip me and I'll show you exactly how that works."

CHAPTER THIRTY-NINE

JULIET

"THAT WAS HEAVENLY." I fall back onto the bed. "I've never had food from Sérénité before."

Kavan adjusts the waistband of the sweatpants he's wearing. "Never?"

Shaking my head, I drop my gaze to my legs.

I'm dressed in one of his shirts again. This one is white, and smells of him. I may just try and smuggle it out of here at the end of the night in my purse.

I want a memory of our time together because even though Nigel says he believes that Kavan is falling in love with me, I won't really know how he feels until I hear those words from the man himself.

"You've been teasing me for hours, Juliet."

I laugh. "Teasing you, how? I was the one who suggested dinner in bed. You were the one who ran into his office to take an important call that lasted over an hour."

There's no apology written in his expression when I glance at him.

"It was important."

"I know," I acquiesce.

I could hear that in the tone of his voice when he answered the call. It wasn't the same tone that he'd used when Harry called or when Nigel calls from him.

He answered curtly with only his surname, before he bolted down the corridor, and slammed his office door behind him.

Dinner arrived thirty minutes later, so I kept it warm in the oven, while I sat at the dining room table staring at the flowers he bought for me.

When he finally emerged, he insisted on a taste of me before we ate.

I offered a compromise in the form of a slow strip tease in his bedroom. He followed that with his own, and before he could get his hands on me, I wrapped his shirt around my body and tore out of the bedroom to plate our dinner.

Dinner wasn't in bed, but it was on the couch in front of the fireplace with the flames of the fire and a few candles lighting the space.

Kavan put on soft music and as we ate, we talked about nothing and everything.

I told him about my sister's business.

He talked about a company that he wants to acquire, and as we sat and drank red wine, I saw the sparks of trust in his eyes.

I glance to where he's standing.

His hands are on his hips, his muscled chest broad, and his face a stark reminder of how savagely beautiful he is.

His gaze is cast toward the bank of windows that stretch the length of the room.

"What are you thinking about, Kavan?"

His eyes stay trained on the endless lights that are in view. "Life."

"Your life?" I ask quietly.

He nods. "It hasn't gone as I hoped, and I don't need you to tell me that billionaires have it easy, Juliet."

I can't tell if he's joking, but I don't absorb it that way. "I don't think they do. I don't think you've had an easy life."

He doesn't glance in my direction. "Neither have you."

Panic spears me, but I take a calming breath. I want him to know, but he needs to hear it from me. My past isn't as complicated as his, but there are moments that I wish I could scrub from my memory.

His hands drop to the waistband of his sweatpants. In one fluid motion, they're pulled down and he's stepped out of them.

I stare at him.

Every inch of him is pure masculinity.

His hand moves to his rock hard cock. He fists it, stroking it slowly. "Do you know what you do to me, Juliet?"

I shrug out of the shirt, dropping it on the floor. "Show me."

This is how he shows his adoration. This is how he expresses his love to me.

He displays himself, physically and emotionally in ways that make him vulnerable.

He's on me then, his hands, his lips, and his teeth.

He dives between my legs, eating me with such force that I cry out when he nips my clit with his teeth.

I tangle my hands in his hair, riding his mouth, taking everything I can from him because he needs that just as desperately as I do.

CHAPTER FORTY

KAVAN

"I'VE NEVER DONE THIS. I've never fucked a woman I've cared this much for before."

I whisper that to myself as Juliet crawls on top of me.

I'm flat on my back in the middle of the bed, and she's hovering above me. I can feel the heat from her pussy and see the need in her eyes. I hear it in her breathing too. It's fast, almost panicked, as she attempts to circle my cock with her hand.

Her eyes widen with wonder as she watches the tip disappear between her folds. Then she lowers herself slowly – so fucking slowly- onto my dick.

I reach up to grab her waist to guide her movements. "Take it slow."

"Slow," she repeats her eyes never leaving the point where our bodies are connected.

"Oh, god," she whispers on a moan. "It's so deep."

I close my eyes to try and stop the need to pump hard.

I want to fuck this woman with everything I have. I want to show her what she means to me by making her come again and again.

I've done that twice already tonight with my teeth and my tongue, but this is so much more. This is the velvet heat of her pussy pulsing around me.

I move carefully, pushing up slowly so she can adjust.

Her head falls back. "I'm going to…"

I pump hard, once and then again, but it's not needed. She's already in the middle of another orgasm. The grip of her around me is too much.

I thrust up again and again, trying to control the need to just fuck.

"Please," she murmurs. "Fuck me."

I take control, spearing into her with solid heavy thrusts.

Watching her ample tits bounce with each plunge of my dick inside of her, I'm mesmerized.

Her lips part and my name spills out dressed in breathy mewls and moans.

"Juliet," I whisper as I feel her tighten again.

Jesus, this woman.

It's so fucking good. Every goddamn time is better and better.

"Coming," she screams as she writhes on top of me, her hands trailing over my chest.

Her nails dig into my skin and that bite of pain is enough to send me over the edge.

I empty into the condom with slow, smooth strokes just as her lips find mine in a kiss that feels as if she's branding me as hers forever.

I WAKE TO AN EMPTY BED.

I turn over to see if she's crawled to the edge of the king-sized bed to give herself room to move.

I crowded her after we fucked.

I tore off the condom, trashed it and then ran my fingers over her pussy until she came again.

When she pleaded with me to stop, I gave in and tugged her next to me.

That's the last thing I remember.

"Juliet!" I call out.

Silence greets me so I glance at the clock sitting on the bedside table.

It's nearing midnight.

With a swing of my legs over the side of the bed, my feet touch the cooled hardwood.

The thermostat is set to automatically lower ten degrees at ten p.m. each night. I like the pinch of cool air on my skin when I rest.

Sliding my sweatpants back on, I take some comfort in not seeing my white button-down shirt on the floor where Juliet deposited it.

Unless she's stolen it, she's still somewhere in this penthouse.

I make my way out of the room, down the hallway and around the corner and that's when I spot her.

Staring into the fire, my beautiful love is deep in thought.

A blanket is wrapped around her body, but her legs are twitching. The rhythmic movement is a sign that she's focused on something.

I saw it before when I glanced into her office to find her typing away on her laptop.

"Juliet," I call out to her softly.

She doesn't respond so I step closer. "Juliet."

Still nothing, her gaze is pinned on the flames as they dance in the darkness.

I don't say another word until I'm less than five feet from the couch. "Juliet, are you all right?"

The answer doesn't come from within her, or perhaps it does.

No words leave her perfect lips, but they quiver and as she turns to face me, I see her tear stained cheeks.

Rushing toward her, I stop short of where she is. My hands fist at my sides, and I exhale. "Who did this to you? Who has made you feel this, Juliet? Tell me. I'll..."

When my voice trails she glances up and into my eyes. "You'll what, Kavan? What will you do?"

I'll kill them.

Those words – those three fucking words – sit unspoken on my tongue.

She darts to her feet and with the blanket in her hand trailing behind her she walks barefoot across the room toward the bank of windows.

I follow behind her. "Tell me what's wrong, Juliet. Did I hurt you?"

"No," she whimpers. "You would never hurt me."

She can't know how much those words mean to me.

"Let me help you." I scrub a hand over the back of my neck as she slows her steps. "Juliet, let me help you."

She turns to face me, dropping the blanket at her feet.

I approach her with cautious steps because I don't know how to comfort her.

"Kavan." My name comes out of her wrapped in a sob. "I need to tell you something."

Dear God, please don't let it be that she's in love with someone else. Please.

I move closer so I can cradle her delicate face in my hands. "Tell me, Juliet. You can tell me anything."

"You can tell me anything," she repeats.

I stare into her eyes. Is that what she needs? Does she need me to speak my truth before she will?

I kiss the corner of her mouth softly before I feather kisses over her forehead. "Trust me, Juliet. I'm not the man you think I am. You can trust me. I trust you."

Her hand moves to my chin. It's the gentlest touch but it soothes the pain that has lived within me for so long.

The urge to speak is almost too much. I want her to know my truth and I want it to be now, before she trusts me with hers.

"I didn't kill him, Juliet." My voice breaks. "I swear to you that I didn't kill my father."

Tears fall from her eyes. "I know, Kavan."

I nod as I swipe the tears from her cheeks with the pads of my thumb.

"I know because I've looked in the eyes of a murderer, and that's not what I see when I look at you."

CHAPTER FORTY-ONE

JULIET

HIS BRILLIANT BLUE eyes lock on my face.

I see pain in the depths of them, when there should be relief.

He confessed what I've always suspected, and I confessed what he never could have known.

"Juliet," he whispers my name. "What does that mean?"

To tell that story takes more strength than I have, but I need to do this.

After we made love, I got out of the bed and checked my phone.

There was a text from my sister, and a missed call, and three more calls after that.

So I put on Kavan's shirt, snuck out of his bedroom and went into my office.

I called Margot and for the first time in ten years she didn't ask where I was or who I was with.

She cried.

I cried, and then we cried together because we are finally free.

I take Kavan's hand to lead him back to the couch.

I sat there, staring into the fire for so long I lost track of time.

He takes a seat next to me with his body turned to face me. He reaches for my hands. "Start from the beginning."

I nod. "I was fifteen."

He shifts his ass so he's even closer to me. "Fifteen?"

"It was ten years ago." I take a deep breath. "Margie was eighteen. It was the middle of summer. Our parents left for vacation. A cruise. It was a cruise in Greece."

Those details don't matter, but they are part of the tapestry of that moment in time. They all weave together to form the memory that I've never been able to shake.

He squeezes my hands.

I glance at the fireplace. "It was raining, so Margie turned on the fireplace that morning. It was electric but gave off a little bit of heat. She had summer school so she left to go to class. I forgot to turn the fireplace off."

"Was there a fire, Juliet? Did the house burn down?"

Shaking my head, I glance at him. "No, no. I just remember that smell that day. It burned all day, until..."

"Until she came home from school?"

I ignore that because she never came home from school that day. The police found her at her friend's house hours after it was all over.

"He came in through the balcony door." I swallow hard. "Margie didn't lock it the night before. We sat on the deck and she let me take a sip of one of our dad's beers, but it was awful."

"Who came in through the balcony door, Juliet?"

I look at his face. "Margie's ex boyfriend. He told her his name was Doyle Creighton."

"That wasn't his name?"

I pick at the hem on the bottom of Kavan's shirt before smoothing it with my palm so it sits flat on my thighs. "His name was Chevy Dorset."

"Chevy Dorset," he repeats.

I look at him again. "Chevy Dorset. He killed two people in Oregon before he ran to California, fell in love with my sister, and then when she broke up with him, he came to our house to kill her, but I was the only one there."

I DRINK from the glass of water that Kavan handed me a few minutes ago.

I was the one who asked for it.

I could see that he needed a minute after I told him about Chevy.

He takes the glass from me to place on the coffee table. "What happened that day, Juliet? What did that monster do to you?"

I reach for his hands and hold them in my lap. "At first, he didn't know I was there. I heard footsteps. They were too heavy to be Margot's so I ran to my bedroom, shut the door as quietly as I could and I called 911."

"Good," he says with a nod as if he's trying to reassure both of us. "Good."

"He heard me."

Kavan's brow furrows. "He heard you?"

"I didn't realize that he was outside of my bedroom and heard me whisper our address into the phone. He kicked in the door to my room then."

"Jesus."

"He had a knife." I close my eyes to shake off the image of that knife. "He demanded to know where Margot was."

"Juliet." His voice shakes.

"I tried to stay calm," I tell him. "I told him we could leave the house together and go find her."

"That was smart," he affirms. "Very smart."

"He wanted me to call her. I tried and tried but she hadn't gone to class. She'd gone over to a guy's house to…she went there to have fun."

"So she never answered the phone?"

"It was hours later that the police tracked her down. It was over by then."

"Over?" He shifts our hands so his are on top of mine now. "How did it end?"

"I thought he was going to kill me," I say on a sob. "But I begged him not to. Hours later when the police stormed in, he just gave up."

He gathers me into his arms then. "Thank Christ. Fuck, Juliet. I'm so grateful you're okay."

"I'm okay." I cling to him. "I'm going to be okay."

Drawing my gaze up to meet his with a finger on the bottom of my chin, he kisses my forehead. "I had no idea you'd lived through something like that. What prison is that bastard in?"

I finally manage a slight smile. "Hell. Chevy Dorset died in prison tonight."

CHAPTER FORTY-TWO

KAVAN

I CARRY her back to bed in my arms.

Resting her carefully on the sheets, I settle next to her.

Face-to-face I stare into her eyes. They are the eyes of a woman who has lived through trauma.

One of her hands moves to cup my cheek. "I'm glad I told you."

"I am too, Juliet."

"That day in the alley when you saved me, it was a lot."

I tug her closer to me. "That had to have been triggering for you."

She nods. "It was. I went to therapy when I was fifteen. It helped. It taught me how to deal with things. Bad things, good things, life."

I know the feeling. I sought out help too after my father's death.

"I wanted to tell you sooner," she whispers. "I was worried that you'd find out on your own."

I'm surprised I didn't.

Before I approached Thurston with the idea of having Juliet write the article, I ran a complete background check on her. Nothing related to what happened when she was fifteen popped up.

"My name was kept out of it publically because of my age," she goes on, "I don't know how far your reach extends though, so there was a small part of me that wondered if you already knew."

"I had no idea."

"We moved after that to a house in southern California with a pool." She smiles. "It was supposed to be our new beginning, but Margot always worried about me after that. She's never been able to let that go."

Her body slides closer yet.

"Thank you for telling me, Juliet."

She looks at my face. "Thank you for understanding."

I drop my lips to hers for a kiss. The intention is for it to be soft and comforting, but her hand falls to my chin to tilt my head.

Deepening the kiss, she moans. "I love kissing you, Kavan Bane."

Groaning, I bite her bottom lip. "I fucking love kissing you."

She moves to rid herself of my shirt so I do the same with my sweatpants, kicking them off in haste.

Her gaze trails over my body. "You sure know how to use all you have."

I huff out a laugh. "That's a compliment."

Her finger wags in the air toward the cabinet across the room. "We need a condom."

I drop a hand to her pussy to run a finger over her seam. "You're right, we do."

I slide to my feet and sprint across the room.

"Why don't you have the condoms in your bedside table?"

I stop just as my fingers find the drawer pull. I take a deep breath, turn and smile. "I've never fucked a woman here before, Juliet. I'm still trying to figure all of this out."

That lures her up to her knees.

Goddammit, she's beautiful.

Her nipples are perked on her full breasts. Her hair is tangled around her face and her eyes are shining brightly as she smiles at me.

How the hell did I get this lucky?

"You have never fucked a woman in this bed?" She bounces slightly.

It's almost too much for me to handle. "Stop moving, Juliet, or I'm going to blow my load right here."

She scurries to the edge of the bed, drops to her feet and rushes toward me.

I stare because everything about this moment in time will be etched in my memory until I die.

When she drops to her knees at my feet, I let out a noise that was born from my desperate need for her.

"We can't waste that, can we?" She grips the base of my cock in her hands. "I have another secret to tell you."

I manage a stuttered chuckle as she licks the crown with the tip of her tongue. "Tell me now."

Tilting her head, she gives me a clear view of her tongue on my cock, before she pulls back slightly. "The scarf may be my new favorite thing, but you are my all-time favorite person."

I don't get to reciprocate that because any words I may have spoken are lost when she takes me in her mouth.

"CAN you write a note to Mr. Marks to excuse me from our meeting tomorrow because I can't move?"

I look over to where Juliet is on the bed. She fell there after riding my cock again. That happened after I fucked her against the wall with her legs wrapped around me and my fingers sliding over her perfect ass.

"You're meeting with Thurston tomorrow?"

One of her eyelids cracks open. "Is there a parrot in here?"

That sends me into a deep-seated laugh unlike anything I've experienced in years, maybe ever.

She moves to sit. "I don't think I can walk. Can you get Alcott to piggyback me to Mr. Marks's office?"

With my laughter fading, I shoot her a look. "Piggyback? What is that?"

"Oh my god, you cookie-cutter billionaire." She jumps to her feet on the mattress. "You're not serious, are you? You know what a piggyback ride is."

"If it involves fucking, I'm going to fire Alcott because I can piggyback you, Juliet. I'm the best you'll ever have."

"You're so arrogant." She laughs. "Turn around."

"I've seen all of that before." I gaze at her nude body. "I'll be seeing it again."

Her hands drop to her hips. "Turn around, Kavan."

I do as asked.

I feel her hands land on my shoulders. "Step forward a little bit."

I do that too.

When her legs wrap around me from behind, I move to kiss one of her palms before I place it back on my shoulder. "This is a piggyback ride?"

"It is when you move," she whispers in my ear. "Take me to the kitchen, please. I'm craving a snack."

I start to move forward as she slides her arms ahead, pressing her chest flat against my back. "Let me guess. Peanut butter and jelly."

"Hell, no." She laughs. "I want some of that honey ice cream I saw in the freezer. I could eat that everyday."

Laughing, I take off in the direction of the kitchen wondering how this became my life and hoping that it never goes back to what it used to be.

CHAPTER FORTY-THREE

JULIET

***Brad:* I have something you need to see!**
Meet me at the usual place.

I GAZE at the text message that just popped onto the screen of my phone. I've been at Marks Creative for the past two hours waiting for Mr. Marks to see me.

I have my laptop so I can show him the article that focuses on the future of Bane Enterprises.

Last night after Kavan finally fell asleep I made the decision to turn in this article. It's not what Mr. Marks wants, but it's what my relationship with Kavan needs.

The other article I wrote delves into who Kavan Bane is as a man. It's a glimpse of him through my eyes. It's deeply personal.

"Juliet!" Shirlene calls to me as she approaches the doorway to what might be my permanent office.

I'm hopeful that I'll have the opportunity to continue to write for New York Viewpoint, but if I get bumped back to covering celebrity gossip for RumorMel, I'll do my best until another opportunity pops up here or with another media organization.

I glance around the space.

It's a lovely office, decorated in soft tones with an office chair that is so comfortable I could fall asleep in it.

I almost did since I only got about two hours of sleep last night before I rushed home to shower and get ready for this meeting.

Margot was gone by the time I got to our apartment but she left a note on the kitchen counter telling me that we're going to celebrate tonight.

I may just ask Kavan to reserve a table at Sérénité for my sister and me.

I have a feeling he can pull a string or two to make that happen.

"Juliet," Shirlene repeats my name as soon as she's in the doorway. "I meant to come see you sooner."

"I'm good." I wave her worries away with a hand in the air. "I've been editing my article, checking all the facts, you know, the usual."

She chuckles. "I've lived the life of a journalist without living the life of a journalist."

It takes me a second to make sense of that. "You must have a lot of memories about some of the biggest stories of the last…"

My voice trails because I don't want to insult her by assuming she's worked here for decades.

I assume she's older than my parents based on her headshot on the Marks Creative website. She must have been in her early twenties then and it is a black and white shot. Perhaps, she was going for a more artistic headshot than everyone else.

"I've worked here a hell of a long time." She laughs. "I've seen presidents come and go. I've witnessed a man stepping foot on the moon. I even got to read gossip about some Hollywood bigwigs before it went to print."

"You're lucky."

"I do have to say that the story you're working on is one I remember very well."

Unsure, if she's trying to get a sneak peek of my article, I snap the cover of my laptop shut. I want Mr. Marks to see it. If he approves, I'll show it to Kavan for his final approval.

There isn't anything sensational in it, so I'm confident he'll be satisfied with it.

Shirlene helps herself to a chair facing my desk. She takes a seat crossing her ankles as she stretches her legs out in front of her. "Mr. Bane was a saint. He went out of his way to help anyone in this city who needed it. When he died it impacted a lot of people."

"That's what I've come to understand," I say, choosing my words carefully.

"I don't think it impacted anyone more than his son."

I glance up to look at her face. "I agree with you, Shirlene."

"The police dropped the charges." She taps a finger against her knee. "I think that says something, don't you? He may not have been cleared in a court of law, but that doesn't make him guilty."

"It doesn't."

"I've always wondered why he didn't speak up and explain the dropped charges." She sighs. "The District

Attorney in Miami didn't get into specifics. Maybe if she had he wouldn't be living under this shadow of suspicions still."

This woman speaks my language. I smile. "Maybe one day he will."

Maybe, just maybe, there are more people who view Kavan in the same light as Shirlene.

My phone buzzes, so I drop my gaze to it.

Brad: **Text me back, sunshine. I'm headed over to meet you on Madison now.**

I PICK up the phone to text him back to tell him that he needs to give whatever he has to someone else, but I don't.

"Shirlene, how much longer do you think Mr. Marks will be?" I wince. "I don't mean to be pushy, but I have a source who wants to meet up. It's close. I'll be back in fifteen minutes."

She taps her forehead. "Damn, my memory is slipping. I came in to tell you Mr. Marks had to leave for the day, Juliet. It's a family thing. His grandson, Penn, said Mama for the first time today, so Mr. Marks wants to hear that with his own two ears. He's been trying to get that little guy to say grandpa, but that'll take some time."

I wouldn't have pegged Mr. Marks for someone who blows off work for family, but I admire that.

"Perfect." I slide to my feet. "I'll go take that meeting."

CHAPTER FORTY-FOUR

JULIET

HOLDING onto the skirt of my dress, I race across the street and to the corner.

Telling Brad in person that I probably won't be using him as a source anymore won't be easy, but I have the name of the newest member of RumorMel's team in my pocket.

I scored that when I ran into Hugo in the lobby of the building.

When I told him about Brad, he handed me a few hundred dollars so I could grab the information if it was worth it.

If it is, I'll drop it off at his office on the way back up to mine.

I race up the sidewalk when I realize Brad is already standing in our meeting spot. He's wearing a bright yellow jacket, green slacks and a pair of black loafers.

The entire look works on him.

"There she is," he calls as I approach. "Looking like a peach on a summer day."

I smile. "You like this look?"

"That's one of Margot's dresses, isn't it?" He points a finger at the peach lace dress I took from my sister's closet this morning.

He should know since Margot treated herself to a session with Trudy to style her current wardrobe.

"And my leather jacket." I tug on the lapels of my jacket. "It's a little Juliet, and a little Margie mixed together."

"It's divine."

I go in for a hug when he spreads his arms. "It's good to see you, Brad."

"I hear congratulations may be in order."

Confused, I look into his face. "Congratulations?"

"You're moving on up to the top floor." He taps the tip of my nose with his fingertip.

"I just saw Hugo." I shake my head. "I know that he didn't tell you."

"Every good source has a source." He laughs. "I have mine."

"Are you going to tell me who it is?"

"I guess she won't give a shit if I do." He shrugs. "It's Shirlene."

"Shirlene?"

"Aunt Shirlene to me." He pats his chest.

"You're Shirlene's nephew?"

"By marriage," he admits. "I do need to tell you that I have never shared anything with her before I shared it with you."

I take some reassurance in that, although it doesn't matter now that my assignments will be less gossip, more news.

"Including today." He holds up a flash drive.

"What's on that?"

"Something you can give to Hugo as a parting gift."

I laugh. "You could have just called Hugo to come get it."

"What fun would that have been?" He scoffs. "I needed to offer you a proper goodbye, although I will dig up some dirt on something New York Viewpoint worthy. You can count on that."

"I will count on that."

He nods toward the alley. "Please come into my office, Juliet."

I shake my head. "I was mugged last time I went into your office."

His jaw drops. "No fucking way."

"Yes." I nod, holding in a smile. "A guy tried to nab my purse after you left."

"What an absolute asshole." He narrows his eyes. "I know he didn't get away with that flash drive because I saw the story about Corla's engagement on RumorMel the next day. Good job on that, by the way."

"Thanks."

"Too bad she dumped her fiancé last week."

I laugh. "You're joking."

"I'm not." He reaches for my hand. "Why don't we take this into the café down the street? I could use a shot of espresso and I'm feeling generous. I'll buy you one too."

I take his hand. "Tell me what's on the flash drive, Brad."

We set off side-by-side toward the café. "Two words. Trey Hale."

I shake my head. "The baseball player who has dated virtually every woman in New York City? Present company excluded."

"That Trey Hale." He nods. "He was at someone's studio with his new girlfriend. This one just might be the one, Juliet."

"It won't," I say with confidence. "I'll give you fifty bucks for the pictures. I'm sure Hugo will run with them."

He drops the flash drive in my hand. "Deal."

"I HAVEN'T HAD a chance to show it to Mr. Marks yet," I hesitate before I continue, "I don't think he'd mind if the brilliant subject of my article had the first look."

Kavan glances up at me. "Juliet, I'm in awe."

I clap my hands together. "You're happy with it?"

He slides to his feet. "I don't know how the fuck you found all that information and wove it together the way you did, but it's masterful."

I glance at my open laptop. "I may still tweak it a bit, but I think it's solid. It sends a clear message that Bane Enterprises is focused on the future and its most recent accomplishments."

"I'm stunned," he admits. "That's not to say that I didn't trust your talent, but this exceeds my vision."

I sigh. "I just need to decide on a title for it."

He nods. "I have every confidence that you'll choose something as noteworthy as the article itself."

"I will."

He grabs my shoulders. "I think this deserves a celebration."

A smile creeps over my lips. "I think so too."

"I can have Nara change the menu for this evening." He glances at his watch. "What do you want, Juliet? What are you in the mood for?"

"Calvetti's spaghetti."

He raises his chin. "That's an excellent choice."

"You've eaten spaghetti?" I tease. "With red sauce?"

He moves to give my ass a pat. "Is this spaghetti dinner going to happen before or after we fuck?"

"I love when you say that word to me."

"Fuck?" he draws it out slowly.

"Verbal foreplay is a thing, Bane. You have the perfect voice for it."

"Is it?" He tugs me closer to him. "Do you want me to whisper something in your ear that will make me more irresistible to you than I already am?"

I kiss his chin. "I want you to whisper something dirty in my ear."

He brushes his lips over my jawline and up toward the lobe of my ear. "I want to fuck you, Juliet. Those sweet sounds you make when your tight little pussy is wrapped around my cock keeps me hard all day."

I tug on his tie to lure his face down toward me. "All day?"

He takes my free hand and cups it around the outline of his erection through his pants. "All fucking day, Juliet."

I give his tie one final pull before I kiss him until we are both breathless.

CHAPTER FORTY-FIVE

JULIET

"WAKE UP, SLEEPYHEAD." I dig a finger into Kavan's ribcage.

One of his eyelids opens a touch. "Another round, Juliet? Let me sleep for five more, then you can sit on my face."

I slap his naked chest. "You can't be serious? We made love all night. I think I slept an hour."

"Stop talking and sleep another hour and I'll make love to you all day."

I press a kiss to his lips. "That sounds divine, but today is the day I turn in my article. I'm going to read it over one last time before I email it to Mr. Marks."

He wraps an arm around my waist. "You still have time. It can't be more than five or six."

I glance at the clock on the bedside table. "It's after seven."

"Well, shit," he drawls. "I need to get up and workout."

"You can sleep in today." I run a hand over his forehead.

"You worked out last night in this bed with me. I'll send the article and then come back to wake you up."

"Why don't you send the article and then come back to sit on my face?"

"That works for me."

"You're a dream, Juliet," he whispers.

I lean down to press my lips to his neck. Inhaling his scent, I close my eyes. "I'm real. This is real."

His hand snakes down my back to my ass. "I know and I never want to let you go."

I stay in that spot, nestled against him, reveling in his words until he drifts back to sleep.

"PASTRIES FOR EVERYONE!" I announce as I stroll into the penthouse.

After I submitted my article an hour ago, I planned on crawling back into bed with Kavan, but he was sleeping so soundly that I didn't want to wake him.

I snuck out to rush home to shower and change. Then, I stopped to pick up another assorted box of pastries to bring here.

"Do I smell something with lemon?" Nigel asks as he rounds the corner from the kitchen.

"Of course you do." I laugh.

He grabs the box from me to take it to the dining room table. "Is Mr. Bane right behind you?"

I spin around. "Nope. I don't see him anywhere and he's hard to miss."

He laughs. "By the way he was dressed when he left, I thought he was meeting up with you."

"He left? How was he dressed?" The questions spill out of me.

He steals a glance over his shoulder at me. "Much like you are now. Jeans and a T-shirt, but Mr. Bane wasn't wearing a cashmere cardigan and his hair will never measure up to yours."

I move to stand next to him. "When did he leave?"

"I passed him on my way in this morning." His gaze drops to his watch. "Thirty minutes ago, I'd say."

Confused, I dive a hand in my purse to find my phone. "Maybe he went to find me? I left while he was asleep. I thought I'd have time to get back before he woke up."

Nigel looks at me with a smile, but says nothing.

I connect a call to Kavan, but it rings straight through to his voicemail. "If you're looking for me, I've been found." I laugh. "I'm at the penthouse. Come home or call me."

"I'm certain he'll sprint here after hearing that." Nigel chuckles.

I glance at the open pastry box. "I can't decide what to have."

"One of each?" Nigel suggests. "It's hard to choose, isn't it?"

Nara rounds the corner with a cup of coffee in each hand. She gives me one before she hands Nigel the other.

I take my first sip. "This hits the spot. Thank you, Nara."

"You're welcome." She eyes the pastries. "You're in a much better mood than Mr. Bane was this morning."

I let out a slight chuckle. "You talked to him?"

"I talked to him," she affirms with a nod. "He didn't talk to me, but that's typical."

Nigel picks up a lemon pastry. "Mr. Bane is not a morning person."

"Is it all right if I steal the raspberry one for me and the strawberry one for Birch?" Nara asks tentatively.

Nigel turns to look at her. "Alcott does love the strawberry filled ones."

Nara smiles. "I haven't seen him since he went down to the garage with Mr. Bane. Did he pick you up from home this morning, Juliet, or was it Drew?"

"I took a rideshare when I left here earlier and another on my way back," I let that slip.

"You were here earlier?" Her face brightens. "I knew there was something there, Juliet. He bought you these beautiful flowers."

My gaze travels over the fragrant bouquets on the table next to the pastry box.

"There is something," I whisper.

"Mr. Bane was in the garage?" Nigel turns to Nara. "Did he take the car?"

"What car?" I ask.

"The BMW," Nigel says casually. "Mr. Bane takes it for a drive sometimes."

"It usually means a few days off for us." Nara laughs. "He drives upstate and takes a few personal days."

Why would he do that now?

I curse inwardly wishing I had woken him up instead of going home.

I press my finger against my phone's screen again to connect a call to Kavan. For the second time, it goes through to voicemail after a few rings.

Part of me wants to run out of here and chase after him, but I don't know which direction to head.

"I'll be in my office," I tell Nigel and Nara as I set off in that direction.

I'll bring in a pastry and some fruit for you to snack on right away, Juliet," she calls after me.

As I near my office door, I try calling Kavan again.

It rings once and then again.

I stop just as I reach the open door to my office.

I pull my phone away from my ear but the ringing continues. In fact, it's louder because sitting on the edge of my desk, next to my open laptop is Kavan's phone.

CHAPTER FORTY-SIX

JULIET

I DROP into my chair and scoop Kavan's phone into my hand.

Notifications crowd the screen including three indicating the calls I just made.

I set the phone down, unsure of what's going on.

"I brought your snack," Nara says as she enters my office. "I'll put it here."

I nod because I can't find the words to thank her.

I feel numb, and confused.

I glance at Kavan's phone again when another notification pops up but I don't read it. That's not my business.

Staring at the darkened screen of my laptop, I see my reflection.

I look nothing like I looked an hour ago when I caught sight of myself in the mirror after my shower.

My hair was wet, my bottom lip marked with a red spot

from Kavan's teeth. My eyes were bright and a smile was stuck on my mouth.

Now, my reflection is marred with concern.

I tap a finger on the keyboard to chase away that sight.

I'm worrying too much. He's likely fine.

Maybe he rushed out to get something and forgot his phone behind.

He probably walked into my office because he was looking for me when he realized I hadn't crawled back into his bed.

I take a soothing sip of the hot coffee before my gaze drifts back to my laptop.

This can't be right.

Panic darts through me as I read the headline of the article on the screen.

My Mr. Bane.

I read the first line in a whisper. "I fell in love with Kavan Bane."

Sucking in a deep breath to try to chase away the approaching tears, I continue, "I met Kavan Bane in an alley. He saved my life. When I saw him again, weeks later, he changed my life."

I read on, silently, remembering when I wrote each word.

The emotion tied to each sentence bubbles up to the surface.

It's my vision of the man that the world thinks they know. It's tender, revealing, and heartfelt. I poured everything into this article.

There's no mention of Ares Bane or his death because that's a chapter in the life story of a man who has pulled himself up from the depths of heartbreak to finally move from that darkness into the light.

It's a testament to the man who deserves to be loved, and is loved by me.

As I read the final word, my hands tremble on my lap.

"Kavan read this," I whisper. "He read this."

I dart from the chair, shove my phone in my pocket, and scoop my purse and Kavan's phone into my hands.

Just as I'm rushing out of the doorway, Nigel comes in and we collide.

My purse tumbles down and all the contents spill out. Kavan's phone crashes to the ground, bounces once and lands face up.

I drop to my knees and sob.

Nigel crouches near me. "Juliet, I'm so sorry."

I shake my head. "No. Don't be."

"I ran right into you." His hands move quickly scooping up my wallet, a hairbrush and a package of gum. "It looks like your phone survived the fall."

"That's not mine." I glance up. "It's Kavan's phone."

He grabs it. "Why do you have his phone?"

"It was in my office." I push to stand. "I think he read something on my laptop. I'm worried that he thinks I betrayed him."

"You would never," he says as he slides back up to his feet.

"I wouldn't." I sob. "There's an article on my laptop about him. It's not the one I submitted. This one is more personal. I'm scared that he thinks that I submitted that one."

His hands reach for my shoulders. "We will find him, Juliet."

"Where would he go?"

"I don't know," he admits. "I do know that Mr. Bane will be back. We need to give him time and when he's ready he'll be back."

CHAPTER FORTY-SEVEN

KAVAN

WHOEVER SAID nature does a body good never got shit on by a magpie.

Fortunately that didn't happen to me, but I saw it right in front of my eyes.

A couple walking hand-in-hand around the edge of a lake got a load dropped on them.

I would have cursed the damn bird all the way to hell, but they laughed. I heard them telling each other that meant that they were the luckiest souls on this earth.

They have that wrong.

I'm the luckiest soul.

Juliet Bardin loves me.

I lean back on the park bench I'm sitting on and stretch out my legs. I drove for hours with the music in my car blaring, and my soul feeling lighter than it has in years.

I woke up to find Juliet missing.

I scoured every inch of the penthouse for her but she was

nowhere, so I doubled back to her office and that's when I saw the open laptop.

I wanted another read of the fantastic article she wrote about Bane Enterprises and our promising future.

I read that, and then beneath it I caught sight of the sliver of another document.

I'm not a nosy bastard, but I saw my name, so I clicked.

It changed my life.

I read that article titled *My Mr. Bane* three times before I stood up in a daze and got on the elevator.

My heart was too full. My head crowded with so many plans for the future that I couldn't think straight.

I pressed the button for the garage instead of the lobby and when the doors slid open I saw my car.

It's always been my escape, so I took the keys from Alcott's hand and headed out.

"Are you feeding the birds?" A gray-haired woman standing a few feet away asks me.

I look at my empty hands. "Not unless they're eating air."

She laughs and glances back at me. "You're a funny one, are you?"

"My girlfriend is a riot." I smile. "Me, not so much."

She walks slowly toward the bench, relying heavily on the wooden cane in her hand. "What's your girlfriend's name?"

"Juliet."

"Does that make you Romeo?"

I look right at her. "That makes me Kavan Bane."

Her eyes flit over my face from behind wire rimmed eyeglass frames. "It's nice to meet you, Kavan Bane."

"It's nice to meet you too…" I hold out a hand hoping to lure her name out of her.

"I never give my name to strangers."

I huff out a laugh. "You know my name, so I'm not a stranger."

That earns me a pat on the knee. "What are you doing out here all by yourself? Where's your Juliet, Romeo?"

"It's Kavan," I correct her.

"I prefer Romeo."

Nodding, I bite the corner of my bottom lip. "I'm trying to figure out how to tell Juliet that I love her."

"Don't drink the poison," she quips.

I laugh. "That never crossed my mind."

"I know the perfect way to do it."

I look out at the vast blue water. "How?"

"I love you, Juliet."

Those words have been running through my mind for days, maybe even weeks.

"That doesn't feel like enough."

Her dark brown eyes scan my face. "You're not one of those cookie-cutter romantics, are you?"

She can't know how fucking funny that it is. I work to hold in a laugh, but I fail.

"I take it you are?" she asks. "Seeing as how you got such a kick out of that."

"I want to be an original romantic," I explain. "I want to do something that will show Juliet how deeply I love her."

She edges herself forward on the bench. "Trust me, Romeo, keep it plain. Make it simple. All your Juliet wants to hear are those three words."

CHAPTER FORTY-EIGHT

JULIET

"IT'S BEEN TWELVE HOURS," I stress to Nigel. "Should we call hospitals? How long do you have to wait to file a police report for a missing person?"

He sets his binder on the corner of my desk. "Juliet, I promise you that he will be back."

I glance at the open page of the binder to see a photograph of a red-chested bird. It's not a robin. It's something else.

"That's a rose-breasted Grosbeak." Nigel taps a fingertip on the picture. "The sounds they make are some of the sweetest I've ever heard."

"I know something that sounds sweeter."

That voice. God, that voice. I have longed to hear it all day.

I look toward my office door. "Kavan."

"My Juliet," he whispers.

"Mr. Bane." Nigel bolts to his feet with his binder in hand. "I'm going home. I'll send Nara and Alcott on their way too."

He starts toward the door but stops when he's next to Kavan. "It's good to see you, sir."

"It's good to know you, Nigel." He pats Nigel's shoulder. "I need you to start calling me Kavan. We're family."

"I can do that," Nigel says in a tone tainted with emotion. "Goodnight, Juliet. Goodnight, Kavan."

"Goodnight," I call as he takes his leave.

Kavan approaches, reaching out a hand to me. I snatch it quickly in mine. "I was so worried."

"I drove north to some lake," he says, pulling me to my feet. "I met a very wise woman on a bench. She helped me find the words that I've wanted to say to you for a long time."

A lump forms in my throat so all I can manage is a nod.

"I love you, Juliet Bardin."

"I love you, Kavan Bane."

"The article." I glance at my closed laptop. "Kavan, I know you read it. I was never going to submit it. I hope you know that. Trust me, I never would have."

"I trust you," he whispers before he kisses me softly. "That's why I want you to submit it."

"What?"

His hands move to cup my cheeks. With his brilliant blue eyes searing a path into my soul, he smiles. "You wrote that from your heart. The world deserves to read it."

"You're sure?"

"Juliet." My name comes out of him sounding sweeter than it ever has before. "I'm forty two billion percent sure."

I laugh. "You know that I never mentioned Ares in the article or that night because that doesn't have to define you anymore, Kavan. You're an incredibly kind, sensitive, and thoughtful man."

"I know." He tilts my chin up with his finger. "I want you to know those details. It's important for me to share them with you now."

"Now?"

"Now," he repeats.

I nod. "Good, but you should know that you have thousands of notifications on your phone."

He looks to where it's sitting on my desk. "That can wait. This is more important."

WE SETTLE on the couch in front of the fireplace.

Kavan places a blanket over my lap even though I'm not chilled.

He takes both of my hands in his and bends his leg at the knee so he can face me.

"We went to Miami for a conference. It was related to a business that my father had acquired a month, maybe two months before."

I nod.

"The idea was that we'd hang out and talk." He shakes his head. "We didn't have a lot of time for that so I was eager to get that chance."

Even before hearing it from his lips, I could tell that he adored his father.

"I had something important to talk to him about," he confesses. "It was a pretty big shift in my life and I needed his approval. That was vital to me."

He takes a second to gaze at the roaring flames.

"What did you want to talk to him about?" I question softly.

His eyes lock on mine. "I wanted to leave the business and go back to school."

"Really?" Surprise taints my tone.

"To study medicine."

My hand jumps to cover my mouth. "I had no idea that interests you."

"It did," he says gently. "Back then, it did. Now, my interest is Bane Enterprises and you, of course."

I smile.

"We had a great day on the beach." He laughs. "He ran into the ocean. I took off after him because my dad couldn't swim."

"You probably can like a champion."

He flexes a bicep. "Varsity team in college."

"Cookie-cutter…"

"There's nothing cookie-cutter about me." He leans closer to kiss me.

I gaze into his eyes. "You're right."

Nodding, he kisses my palm. "We had some shots, some food, walked in the sand, and then he wanted to go back to the room."

"You didn't?"

"There were bikinis everywhere." He shoots me a look. "I was single."

"Ready to mingle," I add.

"Something like that. Before he left to go to the room, I told him my news." He glances up at the ceiling. "I threw it all out there. I said I wanted a chance to pursue my dream instead of his. I wanted to be a doctor."

"What did he say?"

He glances at me again. “He laughed until he noticed I wasn’t laughing.”

“I’m sorry,” I offer with a squeeze of my hand over his.

He takes a breath. “I was telling my father my dreams and an hour later my worst nightmare came true.”

CHAPTER FORTY-NINE

KAVAN

JULIET SITS SILENTLY BESIDE ME. She's giving me all the time I need to confess this to her. I'm grateful for that. I'm more grateful that for the first time in my life, I have someone I can fully confide in.

"I went up to the room after I got turned down by a few women."

"Liar," she accuses, laughing.

"Maybe I turned them down," I admit. "After my brief discussion with my dad, I wasn't feeling it anymore, so I went back to the room to talk to him. I knew he was disappointed that I didn't want to work at his side at Bane Enterprises anymore."

"You wanted to venture out into an adventure all your own."

"I did want that, but he wanted me to carry on the family tradition."

"Most parents want that for their kids, I think."

I nod. "Most parents aren't like Ares Bane."

I pause to gather my thoughts because this is transporting me back to that night.

"It was raining by then. Ares hated the rain." I chuckle. "He used to tell me it was heaven's punishment, so when I got up to the room, he went there."

Juliet moves to cup a hand over the back of my neck. "We can take a break, Kavan. Do you need a break?"

I love her for sensing how difficult this is for me.

I shake my head. "I need you to know."

"I'm right here." Her fingers rake through my hair. "I'm listening."

"He was in tears when I walked into the room. It was a suite. I was heading to my bedroom when I heard him sobbing."

"That must have been difficult."

"It slayed me," I admit. "I felt as though I let him down. I didn't realize the depth of that until I found him crumpled on the floor in the living room of the suite. He was curled in a ball."

Her breathing quickens.

"I picked him up and hugged him. I told him I was sorry." My voice cracks. "I told him I loved him."

I hear a whimper escape Juliet's lips, so I tug her closer. I know this can't be easy for her to hear.

"He let me hold him like that in my arms." I sigh. "He was shorter than me, but just as strong. He pushed me away and starting yelling about how ungrateful I was. He told me he'd worked his fingers to the bone to give me everything and I was walking away from it all. He called me a selfish little bastard."

"Oh god," Juliet whispers.

I drop my head. "He was walking in circles, muttering

about assholes, and ungrateful fucks and sacrifice and his legacy. He raised his voice to scream to me that I was destroying his legacy."

I swallow hard, steadying myself so I can continue.

"I told him to calm down. I begged him to." I squeeze Juliet's hand in mine. "I had to raise my voice to drown out his. I just wanted him to look at me. He'd done it before. He had moments like that when I was growing up, but my mom could always reach him. She could always find a way to get him to listen, but that night I couldn't."

Tears well in my eyes as I think about that moment. That very last moment.

"I approached him. I was crying too by then. I wanted him to sit with me." I shake my head. "I thought of Nigel. I thought maybe Nigel could get through to him. He was with us, but in a room across the hall so I turned my back to go get him."

Juliet sobs.

I do too. "I heard his feet on the matted carpet. It was as loud as the thunder outside. He ran toward the floor to ceiling window and by the time I turned back around I saw him barrel through it."

I drop my head into my hands.

"I didn't think it would break, but it shattered and he was gone."

JULIET BROUGHT ME TO BED.

After I relived the worst moment of my life, she took me by the hand, undressed me, and then crawled in next to me.

She held me while I cried, and while I slept.

I sense a sudden shift in her breathing so I glance to my left to find her eyes wide open.

"You're awake," I say for some reason.

The smile on her face that follows may be the only reason I need.

"So are you," she points out before she kisses me softly on the mouth.

I run a hand over her delicate chin. "That was hard."

"I know." She presses her lips to my palm. "I'm honored that you trusted me enough to tell me."

"I trust you with my life," I say with absolutely no reservation. "But, there's more, Juliet."

"There's more?"

I nod.

"Do you want to talk about it now or later?"

"Now," I bite the word out. "I want you to understand everything."

I close my eyes briefly to gather my thoughts. I hear the soft sound of the lamp on the nightstand being turned on.

The soft light it provides is just enough for me to see her beautiful face clearly. I need to focus on that so I can get all of this out. So I can begin to put it behind me.

"By the time he jumped, Nigel was banging on the door. He had heard us arguing. I ran to let him in. I was panicked. Jesus, was I panicked, Juliet."

"I can't imagine what you went through."

"He rushed in, and told me to call 911. I couldn't think straight, so I ran into my bedroom to get my cell phone even though it was in my pocket."

"That's understandable," she says softly.

"That's when I saw the envelope in the middle of my bed."

"An envelope? From who?"

I look into her eyes. "My dad. It was a note, written on the hotel stationary."

"A suicide note?"

I nod. "I ripped it open and read the first few lines. Nigel was in the room with me by then. I threw it at him and told him to make it disappear."

"It must have been so painful to read."

"Painful, so painful," I repeat. "But, it held secrets. I didn't read all of those secrets in that moment, but I read enough."

"I don't understand," she whispers.

"Ares was in trouble financially. He had run his personal funds dry to keep the business thriving. He was embroiled in an affair with one of his aides."

"Serious trouble then."

I kiss her forehead. "Very and for a long time, I refused to acknowledge that note. I carried the burden of his death on my shoulders. I believed that he had waited to jump until I came back because it was a plea for help, and when we argued that was enough to push him to do it. I blamed myself. I felt I had killed him because I couldn't save him."

"You were arrested for his murder," she says. "Kavan, the note would have cleared you right away."

I look into her eyes. "It would have tarnished his legacy, Juliet, and that was all I had left to give him. All I could do to right my wrong was to honor his dream, so I asked Nigel to keep the note private."

"You're lucky the charges were dropped." She moves to rest a hand on my chest. "You could have gone to prison for life, Kavan."

"I had a good lawyer and they had no evidence of a murder other than statements made by some of the hotel guests." I press my hand over hers. "They dropped the charges, sealed his death records, and it was over."

"People still believe that you killed him, Kavan."

"I know I didn't. You know I didn't. That's all that matters to me."

She presses her forehead against mine. "You have been through hell."

"I survived it. My father didn't," I whisper. "I was given access to my trust fund a few months later when I turned twenty-five, so I paid back his debts, balanced the books of Bane Enterprises and have worked hard since then to preserve his legacy."

"I understand."

"I have never been ashamed of the way my father died," I say with conviction. "If I believed that sharing that note would help someone dealing with mental health issues, I'd do that. The secrets in that note would hurt a lot of people, so I've tried to strike a balance by funding mental health initiatives, and I want to do more. I want to be more hands on."

"I admire that." Her hand trails over my chin. "You're in a position to make a difference in this world."

"You've made a remarkable difference in mine, Juliet."

"I want to keep doing that."

"Forever?"

"Forever," she repeats before she gifts me with a soft kiss.

CHAPTER FIFTY

JULIET

I WATCH Mr. Marks as he reads the second article that I wrote. It's the one professing my love to Mr. Bane.

It's not exactly what he wanted. There are no details of the night of Ares Bane's death. It's simply a journalist spilling her heart out about a man that the world has labeled as something he's not.

"He didn't kill his father, did he?"

I shake my head. "No, sir, he didn't. But I'm standing by that article as written. Kavan's past is his story to tell, and he's not comfortable doing that publicly, so this is my story of who he is as seen through my eyes."

He glances up from his computer. "Through the eyes of a woman who adores him."

"I love him," I say. "Very much."

"Her Viewpoint."

"Excuse me?" I ask because that's a little left field stuff.

I want to keep him on track. He liked the all business

article I wrote about Bane Enterprises, so he may run that. I showed him this one at Kavan's urging. I have my fingers crossed that this is the one that will make it to print.

"Your monthly column in New York Viewpoint, Juliet." He smiles. "We are calling it Her Viewpoint. You'll be interviewing the women who love the wealthiest men in this city."

I bolt to my feet from the chair I've been sitting in. "What?"

"This is brilliant." He leans back in his chair. "What better way to understand a man than to speak to the woman he loves?"

"I'm getting a monthly column?"

"You sure are."

I skim a hand over the front of my blouse. I went totally professional for this meeting. White blouse, black slacks, and black shoes. Kavan insisted that I wear my polka dot scarf for good luck, so I am.

"You have complete control until we get to the final copy." He stands. "You pick your subjects, you craft their stories, handle setting up the photography and then send your column my way by the fifteenth of each month."

I nod, unsure if I can form a coherent sentence.

"We run two months out, so your love letter to Bane will hit the stands in about eight weeks." He bounces his eyebrows. "Maybe you'll be married by then, and we can include a picture of the bride and groom?"

My gaze drops to my empty left hand. "We're not there yet, sir."

"You will be." He taps a finger on the corner of his laptop screen. "The emotion in this piece hit me hard, Juliet. You've got something special to offer to the magazine. It's going to garner us a hell of a lot more readers."'

I drop my hands to my hips. "So my pay will…"

He laughs. "Your pay remains where it is for the next three columns. We'll revisit after that."

"Thank you, Mr. Marks."

"Thank you, Juliet." He offers me his hand. "You brought me something I didn't know I wanted. That rarely happens."

"HEY, MR. BANE," I greet Kavan as soon as I exit the elevator in the lobby.

He glances around. "Can I kiss my girlfriend in public?"

I tug on his silver tie. "You better."

He dips me before he kisses me tenderly.

I have to hold onto him when it breaks because it was that good. "Can I have another?"

Laughing, he leans forward to kiss me softy. "I take it that the meeting was a success?"

"You are looking at a columnist for New York Viewpoint."

"A columnist?" His eyes widen. "Juliet, that's fucking awesome news."

"The best."

"We should celebrate," he suggests. "Where should we go for dinner?"

"Our bed?" I question with a laugh.

"Our bed," he repeats. "I like the sound of that. Is our bed in our penthouse?"

"Our penthouse?" I step back to let a woman approaching the elevator pass me by. She tosses Kavan a look that I can't read.

He doesn't notice.

That's becoming more common. This is the third day in a row that he's ventured out of his penthouse with me.

“Move in, Juliet.” He embraces me. “Live with me.”

I glance up and into his stunning blue eyes. “It’s soon.”

“It’s not,” he argues. “I want it. I know you do, so let’s go grab your stuff.”

I laugh. “You’ll need to meet Margie first, and Sinclair. You have to meet her. She’s becoming a good friend to me.”

“I’ll meet whoever you want me to meet if it means a million tomorrows with you.”

EPILOGUE

3 Months Later

KAVAN

LIFE'S TREASURES are found in the most unusual places.

I found mine in an alley, and now I've found a second at a vintage shop called Past Over.

I wouldn't normally shop here, or anywhere for that matter, but I know that my beautiful Juliet has had her eye on something in the jewelry display case here.

Sinclair Morgan, Juliet's friend, was the one who told me about the ring.

During dinner at the penthouse one night last week while Juliet was busy with Margot and Nara in the kitchen, I asked Sinclair about engagement rings.

The timing was perfect since we were celebrating Nara and Alcott's upcoming nuptials.

I gave Alcott a bonus worthy of an impressive ring. I

gifted Nara the same amount. She told me she was going to sock it away for a rainy day.

That day will arrive in approximately seven months when they welcome their first child.

It's months after Graham and Trina will become parents. Sela Locke is due to arrive right around my birthday. I'm eager to meet my goddaughter and more than ready to tell her tales about her father that will piss him off.

"This one?" The woman behind the counter holds up a tarnished silver band that's barely clinging to a gold-hued diamond.

"That's the one."

"She'll love it, Mr. Bane."

My brow perks. "You know my name."

"Everyone in this city does." She pats her chest. "I read Juliet's column about you. May I say, sir, that you two are a shining example of what true love is?"

I look to the ring before I level my gaze back on her face. "I'm a very lucky man."

She places the ring carefully in a small gift box. "Judging by this, Juliet is very lucky too."

"KAVAN!" Juliet's sweet voice rings out through the penthouse. "I'm home."

"I'm here," I call out to her, just as I place my phone down.

I was talking to Nigel. Profits are up, and he's in Peru on a bird watching mission.

"Very funny. You'll need to narrow that down." She laughs as I hear her heels hit the floor.

She's kicked them off. Her dress will follow as soon as she walks into the bedroom.

I trail her gaze as she skips right past the kitchen on her way to get undressed.

"Turn around."

That stops her mid-step. She spins to face me.

Her hair is down in long waves. Her make-up is just as I remember it this morning when I walked her to work.

The dress she's wearing is a deep green shade and belted at her waist.

I'll never understand how one soul can radiate so much beauty from the inside out.

"How was your day?" I ask casually.

"Fine," she answers suspiciously. "I'm working on a column about Nolan Black, so I met up with his wife Ellie."

I'm familiar with them.

Juliet hasn't requested my help with getting in touch with anyone for her columns even though my connections are vast. She completed an interview with Dexie Jones last month. She's a very talented purse designer. Her husband, Rocco, and I have crossed paths in the past.

I wipe my hands over the apron tied at my waist. "How's that going?"

"Can we talk about that later?" She taps her foot on the floor. "Are you cooking?"

I nod. "I'm whipping up a little something for my bride-to-be."

That sends her eyes to mine. "What?"

I drop to one knee because my plan to make her a peanut butter and jelly sandwich, followed by a scoop of honey ice cream just went to hell.

I can't wait to do this, so I don't.

I yank the ring box out of my pocket.

I took it to a jeweler after I bought it. She brushed up the band, and secured the stone in place. With a quick polish it looks spectacular.

"I stopped living until I found you, Juliet." I look into her eyes. "You not only gave me my life back, but you gifted me with the promise of a future that is almost too much for me to imagine."

Her eyes well with tears.

"I will love you endlessly, protect you always, and respect you until I die. I would be honored if you would marry me."

I pop open the box and she squeals. She fucking squeals in delight and that's all I need to hear.

She gives me more though. She looks past the ring to my eyes, and stares into them. "I will love you forever, Kavan Bane. I will protect you and honor you until I draw my very last breath."

I put the ring on her finger, haul her up over my shoulder and set out for our bedroom. "It's time to celebrate, Juliet."

"That's Mrs. Bane to you."

A PREVIEW OF STARLIGHT

Stars shine brighter when the moon is dim.

I've always been the moon.

That's what happens when you push your dreams aside to fulfill the wishes of the people you love.

It's what brought me to a New York City subway platform with my guitar and a heart full of love songs written from pain and sung with hope.

When Berk Morgan tosses a handful of coins into my guitar case, he accidentally throws in a key.

It's the key to someone's heart.

Berk comes looking for it. What he finds is a connection neither of us can deny.

He tells me I'm his star. He wants me to shine brighter than I ever have before, but that comes with a sacrifice I'm not sure I can make.

CHAPTER ONE OF STARLIGHT

ASTRID

"Hey, blondie. I'll give you a hundred bucks if you give me a private show."

Blondie?

Men in this city are failing – big time.

I ignore whoever yelled that at me because I'm on the subway platform in midtown Manhattan with my guitar in my hands and its case on the ground.

I'm busking. It's the same thing I do at least three times a week when the morning commuters rush through here with a cup of coffee in one hand and their phones pressed to their ears.

On a good day, I'll make someone smile, and I'll leave with a few extra dollars. On a bad day, I'll be subjected to a man in an overpriced suit yelling obscenities at me.

Sometimes I'll yell back because I know that a jerk like that will do the same thing to another woman trying to share her talent with people who need a little pick-me-up.

I skim my fingers over the strings of my well-loved guitar. I've had it for almost seven years. It was a gift on the day I graduated from high school.

I had visions of a record deal and a world tour. My dad and step-mom had a plan that included tuition at a community college back in Ohio. I stuck to their plan until I had a business diploma in my hand. That's when I boarded a bus with the few possessions I had and came to Manhattan.

I start strumming as another train pulls into the station.

The people on their way out of here are a little more generous than those waiting to board the subway.

Maybe that's because they're grateful they made it to their destination without losing their temper or their belongings.

Glancing at the people stepping off the train and onto the platform, I recognize a few familiar faces.

A woman with dark hair and gray eyes strolls past as she drops a dollar in my guitar case.

She's apologized in the past that she can't give more, but I've always told her what I tell everyone who holds guilt in their eyes at the size of their offering.

"Thank you."

I don't busk to make a living. I have another way to earn the money I need to live in this expensive city. I busk because it feeds my soul.

Whenever I picked up my guitar and sang one of my original songs back in Ohio, the people who listened didn't hear anything beyond a pretty melody and lyrics.

They couldn't recognize that I spun each chord and word from my heart.

People who step onto this subway platform hear what I want them to hear. That's a woman who lives and breathes her life in song.

"It's my birthday today."

I smile at the sound of that voice. Lester, a doorman who works at a building on Madison Avenue, stops in front of me.

"It is?" I smile.

He nods.

I launch into a soft sung version of *Happy Birthday*.

Lester sways as I croon his name. I smile when a few people nearby join in as the song nears its end.

Lester claps in delight as I strum the last note on my guitar.

"That's the best gift I've gotten in years, Astrid." He grabs the brim of the hat on his head to tip it forward. "I'll never forget this."

I kiss him softly on the cheek. "Happy Birthday, Lester."

He moves on, disappearing into the crowds of people all racing to get somewhere.

I turn back to my guitar case when I hear the unmistakable sound of coins dropping into it.

I'm met with a gorgeous smile and beautiful blue eyes.

My gaze trails over the man's face. He's handsome. The dark brown hair on his head is messed from the wind whipping outside.

The collar of the black wool coat he's wearing is upturned.

"Thank you." I don't take my eyes off of him. "I appreciate that."

"Have a good day," he says in a voice that catches me off guard.

It's deep and warm. The tone is comforting and kind.

With a nod of his chin, he takes off, following Lester and all the other commuters into the streets of Manhattan.

I watch him walk away, wishing I knew his name and wondering if I'll ever see him again.

Coming soon

ALSO BY DEBORAH BLADON
& SUGGESTED READING ORDER

THE OBSESSED SERIES

THE EXPOSED SERIES

THE PULSE SERIES

IMPULSE

THE VAIN SERIES

SOLO

THE RUIN SERIES

THE GONE SERIES

FUSE

THE TRACE SERIES

CHANCE

THE EMBER SERIES

THE RISE SERIES

HAZE

SHIVER

TORN

THE HEAT SERIES

RISK

MELT

THE TENSE DUET

SWEAT

TROUBLEMAKER

WORTH

HUSH

BARE

WISH

SIN

LACE

THIRST

COMPASS

VERSUS

RUTHLESS

BLOOM

RUSH

CATCH

FROSTBITE

XOXO

HE LOVES ME NOT

BITTERSWEET

THE BLUSH FACTOR

BULL

THANK YOU

Thank you for purchasing and downloading my book. I can't even begin to put to words what it means to me. If you enjoyed it, please remember to write a review for it. Let me know your thoughts! I want to keep my readers happy.

For more information on new series and standalones, please visit my website, deborahbladon.com. There are book trailers and other goodies to check out.

Feel free to reach out to me! I love connecting with all of my readers because without you, none of this would be possible.

Thank you, for everything.

ABOUT THE AUTHOR

Deborah Bladon has never read a romance hero she didn't like. Her love for romance novels began when she was old enough to board the bus, library card in hand to check out the newest Harlequin paperbacks. She's a Canadian by heart, and by passport, but you can often spot her in New York City sipping a latte and looking for inspiration for her next story. Manhattan is definitely her second home.

She cherishes her family and believes that each day is a gift for writing, for reading, and for loving.